Witch of the Red Thorn

DAWN OF THE BLOOD WITCH BOOK 2

Maria DeVivo

Witch of the Red Thorn

DAWN OF THE BLOOD WITCH BOOK 2

Maria DeVivo

4 Horsemen
Publications, Inc.

Witch of the Red Thorn
Dawn of the Blood Witch Book 2
Copyright © 2022 Maria DeVivo. All rights reserved.

4 Horsemen
Publications, Inc.

4 Horsemen Publications, Inc.
1497 Main St. Suite 169
Dunedin, FL 34698
4horsemenpublications.com
info@4horsemenpublications.com

Cover by 4 Horsemen Publications, Inc.
Typesetting by Michelle Cline
Edited by Laura Mita

Library of Congress Control Number: 2022932806

Paperback ISBN-13: 978-1-64450-561-8
Hardcover ISBN-13: 978-1-64450-733-9
Audiobook ISBN-13: 978-1-64450-559-5
Ebook ISBN-13: 978-1-64450-560-1

Dedication:

For Joey – You make all this so much fun. I love doing life with you by my side.

For Aunt Cat (the other Red Sister) – Thank you for always supporting me and for being the best god-mother and auntie. I love you.

For Morgi – It's always for you and always will be for you … just maybe when you're much older.

Table of Contents

Chapter 1

Tuesday, September 20th 1695
The Black Wood Forest
New Haven Harbor, Massachusetts
Night of the Waxing Gibbous Moon

I didn't realize how long we had been out in the clearing of the woods until Tansy's screaming snapped me back into reality. It was almost like a dream—when you fall asleep into that dream world and your story just picks up in the middle of a scene, yet you have all the memory and knowledge of the world that your mind has temporarily created for you. One moment we were walking out into the forest in the purest daylight to gather fresh flowers for the chapel, and in the next instance, it was pitch black and Tansy was pulling hard on my pinafore dress and howling at the top of her lungs for us to run.

"Run, Barbara! Run! Go!" she commanded as I twirled at the edge of the clearing, awestruck at the sight that lay before me—strewn in a circle lay twisted animal parts covered in leaves, muck, and blood. Symbols arranged neatly with twigs,

1

flower heads drenched in the crimson sticky blood, and black candles burned to their nubs protruded from the ground. Something about it enthralled me, bewitched me, and I stared hard at the tableau—unafraid and somewhat curious at the peculiarity of it all.

With one final tug of my dress and a shake to my shoulder, I locked eyes with my sister. Her words finally registered in my head, and her urgency struck deep into my soul: *Run. Go. Now.* We both took off running, my legs swiftly carrying me to presumed safety, my hands still clutching tightly to the cluster of Bellflowers I had previously picked (with no recollection of doing so). When we finally made it to the edge of the Black Wood, the both of us slumped forward, hands on knees, panting hard for air to fill our lungs back up.

"Did you see it? Did you see it?" Tansy struggled to force the words out.

"Yes, Tansy, I saw!" I answered.

"I... I... I thought we were done with all of that! I thought that was past us! I thought..."

"As did I. As did I."

Tansy's upper body shot up with a sense of awareness. Her torso tensed and stiffened, and her face grew dark and contemplative. She furrowed her brow as if trying to piece some wild puzzle together or connect the dots to some great revelation. I saw it glittering in her soft hazel eyes, like words and images dancing in her mind, yet they were too fast for her to catch and put together. When it dawned on her, it was like a candle flame flickering to life. "Today's the 20th, isn't it?" she asked.

"Yes, why?"

She stepped closer to me and lowered her voice. "It's been almost three years, Barbara. Almost three years to the day that Martha Corey and the others were hanged in Salem. You know, the last of the trial judgments. Do you think it's happening again? Do you think what happened over there is now happening here?"

"Hush your mouth, Tansy Wilkins!" I snapped back. "We are God-fearing women of our community. Peace-loving. We reject Satan and all his minions." I paused after those words. For some reason, it didn't feel right for me to say them. A creeping feeling of doubt entered my heart, but I pushed it aside. "Don't you be putting that energy out into the universe," I continued my admonition. "And for God's sake, don't go saying that around anyone else. You know how on edge everyone has been since all that business over there."

"But Barbara, I've heard stories. Been hearing stories..."

"And stories they just are. The same ones I've been hearing too. Nothing but silly ghost tales and monsters under the bed. Now shush, and don't go putting wood on someone's fire. Because the last thing we surely need is what happened *there* to infect us *here*. It's still fresh. It's going to take a little while for that wound to heal." That much was true! I knew our town of New Haven Harbor would never be able to survive the horrors of Salem.

Her face darkened again at my words. It was obvious she wasn't fully convinced by what I told her. I knew I wasn't convinced myself, but I had to say the words to quell my sister's suspicions. It would be a shame if she had opened herself to the hysteria of our neighboring town. Who knows what influence or bogeymen she might allow in? Like a pinprick in the back of my mind, I could feel the scene in the clearing calling me—beckoning me to go and investigate. But I ignored it, and instead, I tried to convince my sister nothing nefarious was afoot.

"Winnie Gordon told me that two young children went missing over in Salem just last week. They were playing at the bottom of the ledge where the witches were hanged, and no one has seen them since. Winnie says those little kids must have awakened something because strange things have been happening since then."

"You know I can't stand that Winnie Gordon. Never could," I barked.

Tansy's eyes went wild. "Barbara, stop that! How could you say that! Winnie has been my best friend since grammar school!"

"And pray tell, why is it that she needed to repeat her studies multiple times? Winnie Gordon is not the smartest of women, now is she? There are at least four, maybe five children in this town who bear the face of her sweet husband Jedidiah Gordon yet do not belong to Winnie herself..."

With a swift shot to the shoulder, Tansy huffed, "Barbara!"

I smirked from the corner of my mouth. "I speak nothing but truth, dear sister. And as for Winnie Gordon, I don't think she could recognize truth if it slithered its way from between..."

She gasped again at my seeming vulgarity. "Barbara! Enough!"

I must admit, I too, was taken aback by the images in my mind and the words that formed on my lips. It was no secret that Winnie's husband was a fine catch for her. A brokered deal between their families to afford the best financial possible outcome for all parties involved. And it was no secret that Jedidiah Gordon was the desire of many of the women in New Haven Harbor, to which he heartily obliged. I envisioned all types of women in our town lying on their backs, receiving the full weight and girth of Jedidiah at once in a passionate ceremony, as if he were a shapeshifter who could penetrate them at the very same time, all at once, thrusting, pulsating, rising and...

I shook my head to rid myself of the thought, but the pinprick sensation was still needling its edge in the back of my head, sending electric waves down my spine. I gave Tansy the bouquet of bluebells and instructed her: "Take these back to the chapel. Someone will probably be wondering where we are and why we're taking so long.

Not a word of this though. To anyone. Not even Winnie Gordon, you understand me. Someone is clearly playing a cruel joke, trying to get everyone excited and spooked for the upcoming anniversary. I'm going to go back to the clearing to tidy up so no one else sees it. I'll be quick and come back with more flowers. Say I was unhappy with what was out there and wanted prettier ones."

Tansy gave a quick nod and went on her way. I turned on my heels and headed straight for the clearing—straight back to the scene of grisly ritualistic murder, straight back to the scene that seemed to call to me, that drew me in.

On closer inspection, I realized the twigs were arranged in the shape of a makeshift circle with the five-pointed star in the center. At each point of the star, a black melted candle was stuck into the earth. The waxy pools at their bases held them in place. A squirrel's severed head was in the center of the star and there was blood—so much blood—adorning the center and outside of the circle.

But the blood sings.

I knelt at the end of the ground altar, entranced with the precision at which it was constructed and thought: *Who could have done this? Why did they do this? What is the meaning behind it all?* But my internal questions were drowned out by the song of the blood and replaced with the only thing I could describe the feeling as—*knowing.* The scene was suddenly beautiful to me, and a wave of guilt tumbled into my soul. I should not feel this way. I should not feel this way…

Yet something in me did. As I knelt to disassemble the symbol and remove the candles from the ground, I felt guilty. As I tossed the squirrel head into the thick of the trees, I felt guilty. As I wiped the fresh blood on the bottom of my pinafore, I felt guilty. Guilty for disrupting someone's sacred space. Guilty for disturbing the hallowed ground. Guilty for…

I shook my head again to stop myself from those thoughts. "What is wrong with you?" I asked myself out loud as if I was expecting some form of a response but knew one would never come. I pressed my hands into the grass to hoist myself up and get back to my sister at the chapel, and as I did, my left palm caught its flesh on a vine of thorns I had overlooked. I winced and withdrew, and in the light of the almost full moon, watched as three little dark red bubbles bloomed across the gentle area between my forefinger and thumb. I pulled it to my lips to instinctively suckle and nurse the wound, and that's when I heard it more clearly, more distinctly. A rustle at first, low and steady in the distance of the wood, that slowly grew to a harmonious crescendo in my head. Music. A melody. A song. An orchestral hymn that lulled me, comforted me.

Awakened me.

I heard it so clearly and distinctly as I gazed beyond the trees of the Black Wood Forest. Its message resonated in my heart and in my head—*something is coming.* I knew I should be afraid. Under normal circumstances, I would have been. But the circle didn't scare me. The candles didn't scare me. The blood and the severed head didn't scare me. It was the thought of being caught out there that scared me. I envisioned poor Martha Corey, Sarah Good, Rebecca Nurse, and Susannah Martin dangling on the ledge with their necks cocked to the side, their eyes sunken in, their cheeks turning pink, to purple, to blue, and I shivered with real fear.

Quickly, I made my way back to town using the light of the moon to guide me to the New Haven First Church of God where Tansy and I worked. We took care of the worship center and the Reverend's quarters—we cleaned, decorated, and occasionally cooked for the larger events when Old Reverend Boone requested. It was a humble yet satisfying calling to be so close to the Lord and to do the Lord's work. Reverend Boone had been a staple of the community for many, many years. It was said that his generational ties to us stem back all the way to England, through his father and grandfather, who were also reverends in their day. But now, with his shoulders slumped slightly with age and his hair completely bald at the crown, Father Boone was ready to retire the cloth. And with no sons to follow in his footsteps, a new clergyman from a neighboring town was set to take his place. Boone had made it abundantly clear to Tansy and me that the church was to look spectacular for the new pastor's arrival.

When I entered the church doors, Tansy and the reverend were at the altar arranging the bluebells among the other flowers that had already been set out. He spun around when the door slammed shut behind me and clapped his hands together jovially. "Oh look! Barbara made it!"

"I'm so sorry," I pleaded as I approached them. "I just wanted to find the perfect bouquet and..."

"No worries, child!" He smiled. "I know your tendencies to overthink the most menial of tasks. That is what the Lord loves so much about you—your attention to detail!" He ran his hand lovingly down the side of my head and smoothed my chestnut braid over my left shoulder.

"Just wanted everything to be perfect," I mumbled.

"I know, my dear. And I am appreciative of your efforts."

Tansy stepped down from the raised stage of the altar and approached us in the aisle. Her face screwed up when she took a closer look at me. "Are you alright, Barbara?" she exclaimed. "You look like you were in a fight!" She said the inconspicuous words, but I knew she was still shaken by what we had witnessed in the woods.

Quickly, I looked down at my scraped-up hands and blood-stained dress. "Oh, yeah. I'm fine. Fell in the bramble on my way out of the woods. It's fine." I nodded tersely at her, silently letting her know there was nothing to worry about.

"Ah!" Reverend Boone sighed. "You two have done more than enough for today. Get yourselves home, get some rest, and I will see you bright and early on the morrow. The new chaplain will be here any day now, and I want everything in perfect order for his arrival."

By the look in her eye, it was apparent Tansy didn't believe me, but I ignored her accusatory gaze, held out my right hand to her, and implored, "Sister?" She grabbed on to me and gave me a tight squeeze.

"Father," Tansy began before we departed, "it truly is not fair that you will not be marrying John and I next month!" There was an irritating whine in her voice that made me shudder.

Boone smiled a closed-mouth smile and folded his hands over his protruding belly like a pregnant woman does when trying to settle down a rambunctious babe in the womb. "Oh, my dear, I promise you, Reverend Gentry will be the perfect officiant for your wedding. He is young and vibrant. You don't want a silly old man like me to guide the first day of the rest of your life!"

"Oh, stop that," she retorted. "You married my mother, Barbara, Winnie Gordon, and…"

"Temperance, I married all the women in this town." He laughed.

"One month. Please. I beg of you. Or let this Father Gentry man take over, but be the surprise officiant for me. It's just a month away. Please!" Tansy nearly threw herself at his knees.

"Temperance Wilkins, John Foster is a lucky man to be betrothed to you. And Reverend Gentry will be the luckiest vicar in all of Massachusetts to have his first duty as chaplain marrying the two of you. Consider it a gift from God. The dawning of a new day. Besides, my child, this will be the first wedding ceremony that I can attend and enjoy! I have waited a long and arduous year for this day to come, and I couldn't see me celebrating anyone else's nuptials this way, save yours. Now, ladies, be off. I am weary and desire sleep. 'Til the morning, peace be unto you."

"And you as well," we said in unison and left the church.

I walked Tansy home to our parents' house, made sure she was safely inside, then continued my trek to my own home. My husband, Douglas, sat in the parlor, legs spread wide with his head resting on the back of the chair. The lantern lights cast jagged shadows across his rugged face, and from the outside looking in, I couldn't tell if he was asleep or not. But I could tell it had been a long day at the Jail House. I could just sense it. He exuded stress and bewilderment that was palpable even from where I stood.

He only turned his head when I entered the front door. "Long day?" I asked.

He nodded. "Long day?" he replied.

I nodded back. "Tansy giving Old Reverend Boone a hard time about not performing her ceremony, the flowers for the new reverend not being proper, the stress of the function to welcome Reverend Gentry..."

"Gentry?" he cut me off, perking up.

"Yes, why?" I inquired.

"Gentry from Mill Cove?"

"Hmmm… not sure. Why? You know him?"

Douglas stood up and walked over to me in the foyer. "Not sure. I don't think so. Something in the name sounds awfully familiar is all." He wrapped his arms around my waist from behind me and buried his face in the crook of my neck. His hot breath radiated up the side of my ear, filling my head with a whooshing sound. It made me wince. Shudder. In a moment that should have sent a thrill up a dutiful wife's spine, I felt nothing but vile spiders crawling in my very veins.

He must have sensed my apprehension to his touch because he pulled me closer to him, practically jabbing himself against my backside. I felt his passion through the thick fabric of his pants and the flimsy cotton of my pinafore, and the thought of him inside me repulsed me. I tried to block him out, tried to not feel his organ grinding up against me, tried to not hear his advances whispered in my ear. I closed off my mind and tried to mentally escape his grip. I envisioned the forest in the darkness. Black sky illuminated by the brightly light moon. The blood of the squirrel smeared in the grass, a five-pointed star forged with tree branches, and the song — the beautiful melody singing to me, calling to me, beckoning me to dance with it in the moonlight. "Not tonight," I managed to say.

He tightened his grip on my waist. "It'll be our three-year celebration in a few days, and I thought we could…"

"I'm not feeling well," I lied, the song still humming in my head.

Douglas let go of his grip and spun me around to face him. His eyes gleamed with excitement. "Don't feel well? Maybe this is it? Maybe you're with child?"

The hope on his stubbly face erased when I shook my head. "It's impossible. I just bled."

He turned from me, stormed into the next room, and kicked the leg of the chair. "Three years, Barbara! It's been three years!" he yelled. "You know after three years, my brother and his wife had two children with a third on the way?"

I followed him into the room, yelling right back. "That's not fair, Douglas! I've done everything you're supposed to do! I've tried to give you a child from the night of our wedding. I promise you. What else do you want from me?"

"How can you give me a child if you don't lie with me?"

Hot anger surged its way to my throat with venomous rage. "One night? I tell you I can't on one night?"

"Maybe you're just cursed," he whispered.

"Me? Maybe *we're* cursed. You know the day of our holy union was the day the last of the innocents were executed in Salem, and..."

"Hold your tongue, woman!" he shouted. "Speak no more of this, lest you dare face the wrath of God and country." He stalked back into the foyer and snatched his coat from the rack by the door. "I'm going out to clear my head. Don't wait up for me." And he slammed the door behind him.

I didn't. I went straight up the stairs, changed into my night clothes, and climbed into bed where I dreamt all night of the Black Wood. I drifted to sleep with macabre music in my ears.

Chapter 2

Thursday, September 22nd 1695
New Haven First Church of God
New Haven Harbor, Massachusetts
Night of the Full Moon

Douglas's words stayed with me over the following days and had me wondering about myself and if there truly was something wrong with me. There had to be something wrong with me; there just had to be. All the other married women in town were plentiful and prosperous in their methods of copulation. Women my age, and even younger than my twenty-one years, who had been wed for even a shorter period, had produced at least one offspring. And he scoffed at me for not lying with him? That was not very nice to hear, for I lay with him whenever it pleased him. One time a fever had raged so fiercely in my body, and he insisted on having me. I resigned myself to the situation because I was taught that's what good wives do, but I was so very sick and weak that it was difficult to move the slightest of muscles. My long brown hair was loose around my face and shoulders, and I had sweat so profusely, strands of it stuck to my skin. I had not the energy to even pin my locks away from my flesh for relief. Later, he had told me he wished I was sick more often—something about heat, sweat, and submission. And he had laughed that I was unable to move and respond. I remember I had thought *there's a cemetery but one mile from here, you can unlock graves to find girls to fall in love with if that's what suits you.* But dare not I say those words out loud!

So, it must be a curse then, because if not, what else? I must be cursed. I always felt it. I always knew something was different about me. As a child, I played by the bluffs of the harbor on the east side of the town. The sea fascinated me. I also loved to roam in the Black Wood on the west side of town—never fearing the woods or the dark or the beasts that lurked within. Mother had called me odd from the moment of my birth.

When the folly of Salem began to unravel and it seemed like the whole world was in a tizzy of a witch hunt, I did all I could to know names and dates and any bits of information I could gather. I was supposed to be concentrating on my upcoming marriage to Douglas Flynn, but it was hard to focus on being a wife and mother when there was so much excitement happening practically in our back yard. Mother cautioned me not to speak of my dark interests in public, to not open the doorways and channels of dangerous chatter, which I was very wise to listen to.

But in July of 1692, when Susannah Martin was hanged in the Gallows, my dearest friend Sarah Hutchings and I stole away for the day to watch it happen. When the box was kicked out from under her feet, Susannah looked over at me from beyond the crowd and smiled. I held her gaze until the light flickered from her eyes and a black shadow encompassed her face into oblivion. Mother was quite cross as she feared for what would happen to me and made me swear to never tell a living soul of what I'd witnessed. Days after our clandestine trip to Salem, sweet Sarah took ill, and sadly passed. Mother said it was punishment for what we had done, and I was lucky I didn't suffer a similar fate.

But what was my punishment? Douglas and I were supposed to marry on Sunday, September 21st, but Reverend Boone was getting over his own illness and asked if we could move the ceremony by one day. A rather peculiar request, but we obliged all the same because Boone was our officiant and longtime family friend, our community authority and grace. It just so happened that the final trial judgments were being held in Salem on the 22nd. Reverend said that our union would be an offering up to God—while the people of Salem were cleansing their filth, the people of New Haven were celebrating new beginnings. It would prove to be a rather auspicious day, and he assured us that Douglas and I would be blessed.

Blessed? Or rather cursed? That was the dilemma with which I struggled. A blessing would have surely brought me a family and a happy husband, but this curse has left me trapped between the prying eyes of the suspicious community and the frustration of my angry husband who wants nothing more than to have an heir. Or heirs.

A knock on the backroom door brought me back to the present moment. I stood in my undergarments musing about my misfortune when I should have been out front making the final preparations for the reverend's farewell service.

"Barbara," Tansy whispered from the hallway. "Are you well?"

"Yes, yes. Just fine," I answered as I threw my apron over my dress. "Fussing with my hair is all."

"Do you need assistance?"

"No, no, almost done, thank you."

"Well, hurry if you will. The whole town appears to be on the lawn!"

I paused and gave a silent inhale of anticipation. "Has the new chaplain arrived?" I asked.

Tansy was silent for a moment, and I sensed she too was anxious. "No. And Reverend Boone is nowhere to be found."

Another moment of silence passed through the door before I smoothed my hands down the front of my apron and opened it wide. I was met with Tansy's sad, hazel eyes, pleading with me to tell her everything was fine. "What do you mean, nowhere to be found? Did you try knocking on the rectory door?"

She nodded, and wisps of her golden hair flitted into her downcast eyes.

I reached out and touched her shoulder lovingly. "He's nervous too," I coaxed.

"Do you think he's … dead?" She gulped.

"Temperance Wilkins, don't you dare speak of such things! You know the power of your words. Reverend just got the communication that Gentry was on his way. He's anxious. He doesn't want to mess this up. This is a big deal for an old man. And think on it—the reverend's whole life has been all this," I motioned my hands in a semicircle as if to indicate the entire world to her, "it must be such a struggle for him to hand it over to someone else. All is well. He'll appear when he's ready."

She breathed in deeply then exhaled every single puff of air so that her shoulders relaxed, and her body seemed to go limp. "Fine," she said, calming down. "Let's go greet everyone outside." She reached for my hand, and we went down the hallway and out the back door together.

The bite in the air was barely noticeable, but I felt it all the way through my apron, dress, and undergarments. It was a chill that was normal for this time of year at night, but for some reason, it was different. It stung. And when the wind gusted up at different intervals of time, it caught me in the throat, stole my breath, and made me gasp for a split second. That kind of wind only happens in the dead of winter when the snow piles high on the ground and a person can barely see their hand in front of their face. But no one seemed to mind, so I kept my mouth shut about it, like I did most everything else.

Tansy was right—the entire community had gathered in the back yard of the church to pay their respects to Reverend Boone. His eighty-year legacy was one of wisdom and strength, and he was an advisor, spiritually and otherwise, to all. This was surely a momentous occasion.

The children played their games of chase while their mothers huddled together and gossiped. When I stepped off the back porch ledge, I felt their staring eyes boring holes throughout my body. Grace Conders raised her hand to cover her mouth as Martha Wiles dipped her head closer, to hear what she had to say. The two giggled as they looked my way again. I turned my body and scanned the crowd for Douglas, but he wasn't there. He was still perturbed from our quarrel the other night and hadn't spoken very many words to me since.

"Goody Flynn! Goody Flynn!" a voice called out to me.

I looked over my shoulder to see Margaret Fletcher and a group of townswomen calling for me to engage them. Margaret was an older, heavy-set woman. Her pink dress was a little too snug around her middle, making her stomach protrude like two semi-circular rolls of bread. When she waved her thick fingers beckoning me to come over, they resembled four ivory sausages dancing above her palm. I gave a slight chuckle on the inside and trudged over out of respect and a little curiosity of what it was she had to say. I soon realized Winnie Gordon was part of Margaret's group, and I think I may have rolled my eyes.

"Oh dear! It's so nice to see you!" she exclaimed boisterously so that the entire lawn of townsfolk could hear.

"Likewise, Goody Fletcher," I returned with a head nod.

"Tell me, child, wherever is Reverend Boone? We've been waiting here for ages! You and sweet Temperance take such good care of him and the church, we figured you would have some knowledge of his whereabouts in his absence and..."

"I don't know," I interrupted. "I know the reverend is very emotional at this time, and I suspect he is deep in prayer and reflection."

Margaret clutched her hand to her chest and gasped. "Oh, why yes, yes, of course! He is entitled to take all the time in the world. I meant no disrespect."

"That's fine," I assured her.

"It's just that the excitement is at its apex, as we await the transference of power, so to speak. We are all anxious to meet the new reverend."

"Likewise," I said again.

"Reverend Boone has been a savior to us all. A true gem of our community. From weddings, to births, to baptisms, to funerals... he's done it all for us. We just want to give him the best sendoff possible."

"Yes, understandably," I said, backing up a few steps to make my exit.

Winnie craned her long neck over Margaret's shoulder. "Someone else is missing too, Barbara. I haven't seen Douglas on the lawn all afternoon." She gave a small smirk.

My blood boiled in my veins and an image of her ostrich neck on the end of a thick rope flashed into my mind. I shook my head to rid myself of the image, and it left me just as fast as it appeared. "He wasn't feeling well," I lied.

Margaret puffed out her lower lip with fake concern and sighed. "Oh. That's unfortunate. I hope he feels better soon. Isn't today your wedding anniversary? It would be a shame if he were unable to..."

Margaret's words were silenced by chuckling. Winnie and a few others raised their hands to their faces to hide their laughter.

I wish you would choke on that laughter, I thought, and immediately my face turned bright red with shame for thinking so.

"Did you hear, Barbara?" one of the other women spoke out. I was so enraged I couldn't place the voice to a face or a name.

"Hear what?" I mindlessly and weakly responded.

"Winnie bears fruit again!" And all the women clapped and cheered.

Winnie rubbed her stomach and smiled. "Just a few months along, but we're happy all the same."

"Number three for you, isn't it?" Margaret said to her. "Come on, Goody Flynn, you must catch up!"

The women chuckled again. Their condescending tone hung heavy in the air. I pursed my lips tightly together and nodded tersely. "That's wonderful news," I said, but there was no inflection or emotion behind my words. "Now if you'll excuse me, I need to see if Reverend Boone is ready to begin."

I turned around and walked briskly away from their circle of derision. I heard their sniggers, laughter, and whispers the entire way as I trotted from the church lawn and the celebration. I needed to escape their hateful, scornful eyes and their evil comments. I needed to go someplace to clear my head and be free from the shackles of their standards.

Tansy stood at the front gate of the church with her future husband, John Foster, and Winnie's husband Jedidiah Gordon, talking endlessly about Lord-knows-what. I tried to rush by them inconspicuously, but Tansy grabbed my arm and pulled me into their range. "Barbara, are you well? Where are you going?"

"Fine. I'm fine. Going to check on Douglas at home. I'll be right back."

Jedidiah stiffened up and grabbed the corners of his green coat. A gust of wind blew his brown hair about his handsome face, and he smiled like the devil. "Take all the time you need with that husband of yours, Goody Flynn," he snickered, "but remember, if you need a hand with *anything*," and at the word "anything" he paused and winked a dark brown eye at me, "you know I am happy to oblige."

John punched Jedidiah lightly on the arm as Tansy's eyes went wide.

"I'll take that under advisement," I said dryly and continued my walk to anywhere.

The Black Wood, I thought. *The clearing.*

I didn't know why, but it was the first thing that came to my mind, so I set out to find refuge in the wood as the sun set upon this terrible day.

The wind picked up some and the sun had fully set by the time I reached my destination. The clearing was clean—free from any ritual leftovers, free from any disturbance of the occult nature. The clearing was clear, and that's exactly how I wanted it. Just me, the trees of the Black Wood Forest, and the light of the full moon peering its head through the branches on its ascent into the sky. I sat on the hard-packed earth and ran my fingers through the blades of grass, trying to release my mind, heart, and soul of this recent sorrow. In and out, my fingers moved as I felt the shards of the meadow tickle the inner parts of my fingers. I drifted. Calmed. Scarcely noticed the wind picking up stronger, like there was a shift in the atmosphere.

Barbara, the wind said, and I jumped up on alert.

Frozen with fear, my eyes scanned the clearing, taking notice of each rustle of the trees, each sound of the animals in the distance, each song of the last of the summertime crickets. In no time, I was fully aware that I was not alone.

"Hello?" I called out beyond the trees. "Is somebody there?" But there was no response, just the cackle of the wind, like the voices of the hanged witches collectively spanning across time. Then something moved in the shadows. I squinted my eyes to get a better look, but what I saw was not possible. A ring, a circle, an ... an opening among the trees, widening, shifting, and glowing, then disappearing as if by witchery. "Hello?" I screamed again, louder; the fear of God rooting me in my place. I wouldn't have been able to run if I wanted to.

And then, from out of the Black Wood, a figure manifested. With outstretched arms, he approached me and spoke very gently. "Be not afraid," he said, and his voice was like the wind penetrating my soul—not a cackle, but a soothing sound that put me at ease. Like a song with a thousand voices not of this earth. Thinking on it, I'm not sure he even spoke the words out loud.

"Who? Who are you?" I stammered.

"Galen Gentry. The new reverend of New Haven Harbor."

My body relaxed and I sighed. "Oh, Father!" I exclaimed. "You frightened me so! Are you lost?"

He stepped forward so that the full light of the moon illuminated his face, and he smiled at me with the most peculiar of smiles—tender and true, yet there was something very sinister about it at the same time. "No child," he said through his full-toothed grin. "Hardly. I was merely taking in all the sights of my new home."

I gave a nervous huff. "We've been waiting patiently for your arrival. The whole town is ready to greet you. I'm Barbara."

"Yes, Barbara Flynn. Reverend Boone has told me much about you. I do hope you'll stay on as church hand, as dear Henry says you are a true treasure."

"Oh, yes. Of course, of course," I said without hesitating.

He reached for my hand and gripped it tightly in his, and like a static shock, my arm instantly tingled. He stared into my eyes, a knowing look that made me blush and squirm. His gray eyes were hypnotizing, and I got lost in them—in the clouds, swept away in their storm. I melted into them, transforming my shape and entire being. His eyes oozed into his soul like hot water bubbling through his veins. My heart fluttered and stopped for a fraction of a second, and I found it so very hard to catch my breath.

"Barbara, are you well?" he asked.

"Oh, yes. Yes. Everyone keeps asking that of me today."

"Rightfully so, you look perplexed, troubled."

I tucked my head to my shoulder sheepishly. "Is it that obvious?"

He gave a hearty chuckle. "Slightly."

I giggled back like a silly schoolgirl.

"As your pastor now, you know you can come to me with any of your grievances. Whatever vexes you, I am here to guide you in the ways of the spiritual, emotional, and physical."

"Thank you, Father," I answered. "That means so very much to me."

"Barbara, you are a child of God," he said as he wrapped his arm around my shoulder and enveloped me close to him, "and I hope to work very closely with you to set you on the right course. Do not let the words of those women trouble you so. You are so much better. Destined for greatness. I see it in you."

My body fit perfectly under the cloth of his pastor's cape, and before I could question how he knew about the womenfolk, a wave of light washed over me and filled me with an indescribable sensation. It pulsated throughout my entire body—from the crown of my skull, to the inner most pleasure points in my loins. I was so quickly enamored with his presence and light that I did not want to leave his side.

"Father, would you like for me to lead you to the church from here? It's not very far, and I am familiar with the way."

"Galen. Please call me Galen when we are alone together. No need for such formalities when we will be working side by side. And it won't be necessary. I know the way. Besides, you have other business to attend to."

"Other business?"

"Douglas waits for you at home. Go to him. Make things right."

How did he know? I thought, but I was so completely drawn to him that the thought barely registered.

I looked up to his chiseled face. The finely drawn jaw, the slightly protruding cheekbones. Small lines at the corners of his eyes let me know he couldn't be much older than thirty, which was only nine years my senior at most. It suddenly felt strange to call him Father. "Yes, Father, I mean, Galen. I understand. I will do as you command," I said before leaving his side and heading for home.

There, Douglas was awake in our bed, like Galen had said he would be. Naked under the duvet, eyes wide open, body glistening in the candlelight. There was a sorrow in his eyes, and a longing, with a spark of a passionate fire. I walked across the creaky wooden plank floor, made my way to the bed, and reached my hand under the cover to gently stroke his body from legs to chest. He shivered with delight and pulled me on top of him without saying a word. Nary a word did I say as well, and as I performed my wifely duties on this auspicious day of our third wedding anniversary, I couldn't help but imagine myself bucking wildly against the most esteemed Reverend Galen Gentry who had sauntered out from the blackness of the Black Wood and somehow ended up in my bed.

Chapter 3

Friday, September 30th 1695
Goody Olson's Home
New Haven Harbor, Massachusetts
Morning of the Night of the Last Quarter Moon

O ld Reverend Henry Boone died last week. To be more precise, he passed away the very night Reverend Gentry came to town. When Gentry had arrived at the church, Tansy told me of the absolute frenzy that swarmed about him. She said it was like a magnetic life force had bewitched the whole congregation, and there were questions and praises, and lots of doting over our new pastor. She said time stood still in a maelstrom, and it wasn't until hours later when someone finally opened their eyes and asked about Reverend Boone. Unfortunately, Tansy's suspicions were correct as they found him in his chambers slumped over onto his bed in a state of undress. He was cold to the touch, but they said there was a smile on his face. Certainly, he had made peace with the transference of power. Boone's entire life had been in service to the Lord and to the people of New Haven, so it was no surprise that he would depart this humanly world when he no longer was the priest holder.

At Reverend Boone's funeral ceremony, Tansy expressed to me her deepest feelings of guilt and responsibility. "He was a dying old man," she said. "We should have checked on him to make sure he was alright. How could we have all just forgotten about him like that? It was my fault! I put the idea of his death into the universe."

Luckily, I was able to quell her fears. "There was nothing we could do," I assured. "If we did know, then what? Were we to save his life? No. It was his time to go home to the Lord. And trust me, Tansy Wilkins, you had nothing to do with his passing. When it's your time, it's your time."

That seemed to calm her down. It diverted her attention and made her inquire about something else ... my whereabouts the night Boone died. I explained how I had met Reverend Gentry (although I left out the part about being in the woods), how he counseled me, and how I went back home to be with Douglas. She naturally responded with a silly giggle of unease that bore a hint of shame and interest. With her own nuptials taking place in less than a month, I knew she was all-too curious about what happened inside a wedded couples' bed chamber. Her innocence flushed hotly on her porcelain face. I also told her that I had been feeling strange on the inside. It felt as if there was a pulling and tugging coming from my insides.

"I think it's possible I'm with child," I said to her as we walked down the road to the church together.

"Hmmm..." she pondered, placing her long, slender finger under her chin. "I don't know much about all that. I am not knowledgeable in the ways of desire; however, I don't think it works like that, Barbara. Wouldn't it be too soon to tell?"

"Yes, certainly. Normally. But I'm not feeling normal by any means. I'm not feeling like myself. I feel..." I paused, struggling for the words. "Energetic. *Charged.*"

"Well, isn't that contrary to the feelings of the expectant? Every woman I know with a swollen womb is anything *but* energetic!"

I touched my lower abdomen lovingly and dreamed of a life springing inside of me. I smiled at the thought. "I know, I know. It's just... this is different. I don't know how, and I don't know why, but this is *something.*"

"Have you said anything to Douglas about this?"

"Oh, heavens no! Not a word! I wouldn't do that to him unless I was perfectly positive."

"Have you mentioned this to anyone else?" she inquired.

I sighed and tucked my hair behind my ears. "I had thought about mentioning it to Reverend Gentry."

Tansy made a little gasp in her throat. "Don't," she blurted.

I furrowed my brow hard and deep until my eyes felt like hazy slats on my face. "And pray tell, why not?"

She threw her arms wildly in the air until her hands came slapping down on the tops of her thighs. "I don't know. Doesn't Reverend Gentry give you a kind of spooky feeling?"

Now it was my turn to gasp. "Tansy Wilkins! Whatever do you mean? Reverend Gentry has been nothing but sweet, kind, supportive, and helpful. He's truly opened my eyes to a new outlook on life."

"Embellish!" she huffed.

"Praiseth the Lord, Tansy! Reverend is a gentle and loving man."

"His eyes are peculiar, Barbara!" she continued. "Haven't you noticed that they change colors?"

"*Embellish!*" I hollered, throwing her word right back at her. "That's impossible. Different lighting reflects the myriad of colors. Changing colors, pshhh! That's the craziest thing I've heard."

"I don't know," she relented. "Don't you think he's too handsome to be a reverend?"

I looked down at the dirt beneath my feet and kicked some rocks to the side of me. "Ahhh," I sighed. "It's too bad he's devoted to the cloth, now isn't it?" A huge smile crossed my face, one that caught Tansy's attention and prompted her to swat my elbow.

"Barbara Flynn!" she admonished with her mouth opened wide. Her hazel eyes nearly bulged from their sockets. "Such words! Such words!"

Chapter 3

"I jest, I jest," I laughed, and she loosened up and laughed right along with me. But there was some truth hidden behind that joke. I had often thought of Galen Gentry with lustful desire. Dreamt of him. And the mere thought of being in his presence made me swoon with profane passion. But I tucked those feelings away with nary a word spoken out loud.

After a block or two, we came upon the home of Goody Olson, the New Haven Harbor midwife. Widowed in her early years, Goody Olson never remarried, nor did she ever have children of her own. She devoted her entire life to ushering into this world all the dear and fair souls of the town. She was aged, yet spry, and quite capable. Her natural talent for caring for the expectant, delivering the newborns, and teaching new mothers the art of motherhood was renowned throughout the community. She was a master of her craft, but there were other stories about Goody Olson that no one dared speak.

I grabbed Tansy's hand and dragged her to the porch.

"What are you doing?" she questioned.

"Come with me. I want to speak with her." I nodded my head in the direction of the front door.

Tansy's eyes narrowed inquisitively.

"If anyone would be able to tell me true, it's Old Goody Olson."

"No, Barbara. It's too soon," she said and gave my grip a little resistance.

"She's the midwife, Tansy. There's no reason for your hesitation. She'll check me out and give me a yay or a nay. It's her job to do those things."

She shook her head. "No. That's not why you want to see her. It's too soon. She won't be able to tell yet. Besides, you know what they say about Goody Olson..."

"Don't even say it. Don't even put it out there. She knows things that were passed down from the Old Country, that's all. Things that women did to get by ages hence. Didn't Mother ever tell you of the herbal tincture Goody Olson made when you were still in her womb and how it eased Mother's sickness? Or how when Goody Bedford's newborn babe struggled to take its first breath, how Goody Olson prepared a stew and let the steam from the pot open the child's passageways? Philip Bedford is strong and healthy now. Endless upon endless stories. You've heard them all. And besides, when you're with child, who will you need to consult? Goody Olson. That's for sure. And you know how long I've waited for this. I just need to know." My eyes pleaded with her, and I knew she couldn't deny me my request.

She relaxed her hand and hung her head low. "Fine, Barbara. Fine."

Goody Olson heartily opened her door and let us in. Her eyes brightened when she saw me, and she quickly scooted us into her home. "It's been a long time in the making, hasn't it?" she said to me.

Chapter 3

"Well," I answered, "that's why I'm here to find out." Tansy glared at me from the corner of her eyes. I could feel her tension mounting.

She motioned for us to follow her deep into the house. "Come. I have an appointment, but not for an hour or so."

I had never had a reason to be in Goody Olson's home before, so this was my first time. The inside was dark, even in midday, and a pungent aroma permeated throughout. Roses? Burning wood? Sage? I couldn't quite identify the combination of smells. Walking through the narrow hallway, the wooden floor creaked with a loud ferocity that made both Tansy and me flinch. Goody Olson gave a small laugh. "Old home. Old things," she commented. "The house speaks. You just need to listen." Tansy and I glanced at each other, and I began telling my story and timeline to the old midwife.

She led us to the back end of the rickety house and sat us at a round table in the center of the room. I had thought it would have been an examining room with a bed and medical supplies. I was fully prepared to undress and allow the midwife to poke and prod deeply into my nether region, but instead we convened in what seemed to be her library. The room was dark, not quite black as pitch, as it bore no windows or doors, just the one from whence we came through. Shelves of books adorned every wall. She quickly scurried around lighting candles at each corner of the room and at the center of the table, creating a soft orange glow throughout. Many tools were laid out before us, items that were unfamiliar and unusual to me. Tansy squeezed my knee underneath the table, and I gently rubbed the top of her hand to indicate that all was well.

"Will you be examining me?" I asked, and the words sounded so trivial as soon as they left my lips.

"Oh no!" Good Olson exclaimed. "It's way too soon for that."

Tansy kicked my shin. "Told you," She muttered under her breath.

Goody Olson sharply looked to her and lowered her brow. "But there are other ways. There are markers to indicate whether or not life springs in your womb."

"Yes, ma'am, please!" I cried out anxiously. "I am so very eager to know."

Goody nodded her head in acknowledgment. "Of course you are. Of course. Just understand my methods are not foolproof. There is a margin of error, as with anything."

"I understand."

Tansy's head spun around to observe the oddities in the room—hanging herbs from the threshold, glass jars with colored liquids, small monument-like structures compiled of bones. Her neck stopped at mid-angle, and I felt her body tense from under the table. I too, craned my neck in the same fashion to observe what had made her blood run cold.

"Is… is that…" she stammered and pointed to the bookshelf.

I strained my vision in hopes of seeing more clearly. Books lined up neatly against each other, all with strange titles and lettering. A bold "B" stood out, but I could scarcely see the rest of the title. I struggled and inched my body forward to see better, but Tansy pointed at a book and distracted me.

"*Malleus Maleficarum?*" she stuttered.

"Ahhh, yes," Goody Olson sighed.

Tansy was frantic, her breath came in labored pants. "But… but… that's the…"

"Yes dear, the book that Tituba owned. A funny story, it quite is," Goody began. "She really brought the devil to Salem, didn't she?" and she gave a small huff of a laugh. "It was confiscated upon her imprisonment and held in the chambers of Governor Phips at the time. When he left office last year, he bid me have it. He had no use for it and fearing it would get into the wrong hands and perpetuate the hysteria, he entrusted it to me, being a distant cousin of mine and all." She paused and gave a long thoughtful look at Tansy. "Come to think on it, Temperance, your betrothed, John Foster? Isn't he kin to Ann Foster of Andover? The confessed old witch whom the devil visited in the form of a bird? Hmmm… seems anyone can point a finger in these parts. Seems the devil lurks in the darkest of corners. Seems witches all over choose to lie with those devils and do their bidding."

Rattled, Tansy placed her hands on the table and stood up abruptly. "I'll be outside waiting, Barbara. Come when you're finished in here. G'day, Goody. I can see myself out." She didn't even look at me upon leaving.

As if Tansy had never been in our presence, Goody Olson reached her hand across the table and wiggled her fingers at me. "A lock of hair, please. Plucked from the root."

I obliged, fished underneath my white laced cap, pulled out a thick, brown strand from the top of my head, and handed it over to the midwife.

She held it out in front of her face, investigating it in the candlelight. Then, she picked up a pointed wooden stick at the table and tightly wound the hair around it. "Give me a finger," she instructed, and when I did, she used the pointed edge of the rod to prick my finger. A blood bubble bloomed at the tip, and I winced. "Now, now," she coaxed, squeezing my finger so the blood rose higher from the flesh. Goody moved a small ceramic bowl underneath my finger to catch the droplet. Inside the dish was a thin white crystal covered with a clear liquid, although I couldn't tell if it was water or not. She shook my finger three times over the bowl so that three droplets of my blood splashed within. "Relax now," she instructed and dangled the stick with my hair wrapped around it over the dish. The stick spun around and around, and as I watched, the three drops of blood separated into three little dots, then combined to form one small pool in the center of the dish on top of the crystal. Goody clasped her hands together and stood, bidding me to rise as well. She embraced me and congratulated me.

"I am?" I asked.

"Seems you are." She smiled, and I returned the facial gesture.

Still in Goody Olson's embrace, the book on the shelf came into my view again. The one with the "B" next to the *Malleus Maleficarum*. "Blodhek-sa?" I sounded the word out loud.

Goody pulled from my embrace and gave me the strangest look. "What did you say?"

"That book, over there," I pointed. "What's *Blodheksa*? Curious. It's not in English. What is it?"

She held me at arms-length and eyed me up and down. Then she placed her hands on my lower abdomen and paused, as if she were feeling for something. Or *listening* for something.

"You can see that book?" she asked suspiciously.

"Of course, I can see it," I said exacerbated. "It's right next to Tituba's and…"

"No one can see that book, Barbara," she said, lowering her voice. "That book is cloaked."

I didn't understand the words she said to me. "Cloaked? What do you mean, cloaked?"

"It doesn't exist. It's not there," she said, touching my stomach again.

Not in this realm. I heard Goody's voice say, but it wasn't out loud. Her voice penetrated my head, as if it had invaded the front part of my brain and traveled to my ears.

She walked over to the book and removed it from the shelf. The cover read *Blodheksa, Blodbrødre, og Blodsøster.* "Read it," she demanded as she held it in front of my face.

The letters were familiar as I had known them to be from the English language, yet they were arranged so oddly, as if they were not from this land.

Not from this realm.

I tried to pronounce the words as accurately as I could, and by the look on her face, she was both shocked and pleased. She then opened the book and fanned the pages before me. A sharp wind caught in my throat, and I nearly choked on the scent of ancient paper—dull and dry, with a moldy undertone like dirt from an old grave.

There's a cemetery but one mile from here. You can unlock graves to find girls to fall in love with if that's what suits you.

"Can you see the pages? Can you see what is written within?"

She waved the book around again, and I nodded fervently. Yes, I could see the writing, but the words meant nothing. Nary a word I could decipher with knowledge of its definition.

Not of this realm.

She closed the book and placed it gingerly into my hands. Her eyes shone with a fire of a thousand candles, and her face illuminated with joy. "It is yours," she said solemnly. "It has always been yours."

Chapter 3

"I... I don't understand," I stammered, confused and taken aback.

She placed a hand on the book and a hand on my abdomen, and she smiled brightly. "Keep it close to you. It holds the words of the ancients—of a land of ice and snow, and a people of the darkness. For you are the only other one to whom it has revealed itself. The blood brother and blood sister."

"But what does it say? What does it mean?" I asked, bewildered.

"It says what it needs you to hear. Its meaning will reveal itself to you." She pressed her hand more firmly against my womb. "Three." She smiled.

She held my gaze for what felt like an eternity, and I stared into her eyes with a sense of wonder and knowing. And in that time, in that brief forever, the color that was within her eyes sang and danced...

And changed.

Chapter 4

Friday, September 30th 1695
Goody Olson's Home
New Haven Harbor, Massachusetts
Afternoon of the Night of the Last Quarter Moon

A fter a little while, I placed the book in the front pouch of my apron and wrapped my knitted sweater around my body to try to conceal the thickness of the book bulging from my clothes. The last thing I wanted was an already cross Tansy prying her eyes into something I knew would only fuel her anger and disdain. With one final squeeze of my hands, Goody Olson bid me farewell and sent me on my way out the front door.

My heart sang and my head swam from the events that had transpired, and I placed one hand on my womb and one hand on the book as beautiful thoughts and images of all of life's possibilities swarmed like honeybees in my imagination, but when I stepped off the porch, my euphoric state came to a crashing halt for standing at the rickety wooden gate was Tansy and Winnie.

Winnie's eyes went wide in mock surprise when she saw me coming toward them. "My dear! A visit with Goody Olson?" she gushed.

"Hello, Winnie," I said and quickly turned my attention to Tansy. "We must be going. Service is in a few hours and Reverend will need us to set everything up."

Tansy nodded her head sharply. "Yes," she said then looked to Winnie. "We'll talk later."

"Sure, sure," Winnie answered. "And Barbara, I hope you got the answers you were looking for." Her voice was melodic and sweet, but it was untrue and sickened me.

"Thank you," I replied weakly and turned on my heels.

But Winnie wasn't finished fishing. "Oh, Barbara," she called to me, and I spun back around with a questioning expression on my face. "I surely hope that whatever you and your husband do is working out for you, because the last thing we need is a harlot running around the streets, bewitching all the good and decent married men in town."

I paused, took a step forward, not fully understanding the extent of the words coming from her sour mouth. I could feel Tansy freeze up next to me. Her whole body stiffened with fear. "Excuse me?" I inquired.

Winnie pursed her lips and raised her brow with an admonishing expression. "I'm not saying what a hundred other people haven't said before.

If it was Douglas who was the problem, it might lead you to do unthinkable things to give you reason to come visit Goody Olson. And if that's the case," she stopped, shifted her hand to her hip and rocked her body in place as if she were wagging her whole self in my face, "then you should just remain the barren old crone and devote yourself to something other than your pursuit of family."

A small squeaking noise escaped from Tansy's throat, and my eyes flashed with a red fire of anger and hatred.

"Excuse me?" I repeated and took another step forward. "I'm not quite sure I understand what you're implying." But I did. And I wanted to hear the words from her mouth directly. I wanted her to say it true and straight.

Winnie gave a slight, condescending chuckle, but she backed up a step and tried to position herself to make her way up the steps of Goody Olson's porch. "Come now, Barbara," she said motioning her hands in the air in a downward fashion. "Jedidiah told me you damn near propositioned him the other night at Reverend Boone's send-off party. And if it were any other woman, I would have been raging with anger, but alas, it was poor, sweet Barbara Flynn—just a lost, motherless soul grasping at everything possible to accomplish her dreams."

I balled my fist with blind rage, and I must have taken another step toward her because Tansy reached out and grabbed my elbow to prevent me from getting any closer to her. Tansy called my name quietly from the corner of her mouth in hopes of calming me down and breaking me out of my heated state.

"Is that what he told you, is it?" I sneered and placed my hand instinctively on top of the *Blodheksa* book that rested nestled atop my thigh. "But isn't it his bloody seed between your legs?"

Tansy and Winnie twisted their faces at my strange words. Honestly, I'm not even sure what they meant or why I said them. I was about to say something else about her husband being unfaithful to her, but when I opened my mouth to say the words, they didn't come. In my mind I thought: *And have you spoken to Goody McDonough? Or Goody Walters? Or Goody Jones? Because they have five children among them who seem to favor your dear Jedidiah. Seems the real harlot has been under your very nose for years!* Then the images in my head appeared. I clutched the book tighter as I saw Jedidiah Gordon mounting McDonough, Walters, and Jones in my imagination. But they were twisted and dark images. All four of them tangled in a matted mass of rose thorns. He snarled as he thrust into their bodies, busting them wide open and spilling his venomous seed into their loins. I envisioned him as a goat, bucking wildly into their backsides, his cloven hooves tearing at the flesh of their shoulders. And then, I saw Winnie with her legs spread wide open, her private area in full view, and Jedidiah, as the goat, rammed her deep in her crevice with his horns as if to pleasure her there with his stabbing motion. She moaned from the sensation, reaching her pinnacle, but he pulled out the horn leaving behind a bloody mess of gore and baby body parts.

Winnie gasped and clutched her chest, her scared eyes confused and distraught.

"Barbara, she's pregnant," Tansy whispered, as to stop me from saying anything else to attack Winnie and her unborn child. But it was done. For I said nothing, yet somehow, I had the feeling that she, too, *saw*.

In a flash, Goody Olson was at the door with a questioning eye. "Goody Gordon?" she called. "Let's get you in for your appointment, dear."

"Yes, ma'am," she muttered, and Tansy and I walked away in silence.

Reverend Gentry was magnanimous that afternoon, and there was an energy that pulsated and radiated throughout the church. It seemed the entire town was there for the service, and Reverend's sermon had brought on many cheers of "amens." Tansy and I had set up the church just right with roses and bluebells adorning the vases at the altar and the candles spaced out perfectly to give the inside just the right glow against the backdrop of the setting sun. Douglas met me there straight after work and sat beside me in the front row like he usually did. He rested his hand in my lap. My insides were bursting with happiness as I was anxious with joy to tell him of our good news. I smiled from ear to ear as I placed my hand over his. There was a dreamy gaze in his eyes every time he looked over to me. Loving. Connected. I was content to know that we were finally going to start our life together as a family, not just as man and wife but as mother and father—a part of ourselves taken and shaped to create something familiar, yet new.

Unfortunately, Reverend's sermon was lost on me, as I sat there dreaming of cradling a newborn babe at my breast. I closed my eyes and could feel its soft skin against my fingers and smell its baby scent under my nose. And when it cried, I didn't care, because just hearing the sound meant it was alive and real, and I would do anything and everything to protect it so. "What is the baby?" someone would ask. "Just a baby," I would answer. "What is its name?" someone would ask. "Baby," I would answer.

I swooned at the thought.

"...and remember, keep your good thoughts flowing and your actions to match!" Reverend's closing words broke into my daydream, and I blinked a few times at Douglas. His eyes smiled back at me, and we rose from the pew to join the rest of the congregation out back. The sun was slowly descending off the horizon, and there was a purple glow in the late September sky. Bats chattered overhead, and other woodland creatures began to rustle in the area. Tansy caught my attention from the back door, signaling for me to help her distribute the light refreshments.

I released my hand from Douglas's grip. "Let me get to work," I said, and as I turned around,

Reverend Gentry was right there, I nearly bumped into him. "Oh, Reverend!" I gushed, startled.

He laughed heartily. "It's fine, child. It's fine."

The three of us giggled awkwardly.

"So," he began, "what did you think of today's sermon?" He smirked a side smirk and tilted his head slightly to the side like he was giving me a knowing look. Douglas didn't take notice of this gesture, but I did—it was meant for me.

I stiffened. I couldn't recall one thing about the sermon due to my incessant daydreaming, but something told me it was acceptable, so I gave him a little smirk back.

"Very engaging," Douglas answered. "You brought together many concepts and gave the entire congregation much to ponder."

It was a cold and generic response. I don't think the Reverend was fully convinced of Douglas's sincerity, and he turned his attention to me. "Distracted a little today?"

I tightened my lips together and nodded. I couldn't necessarily lie to my priest.

"Well, I can't argue with that." He sighed with a smile. "There is much to be distracted about." And he reached his hand out to touch my abdomen. The palm of his hand was flat against my stomach, but the tip of his forefinger caressed the spine of the book in my apron pocket.

Douglas pulled back, wide eyed. His face twisted to the side with a puzzling gaze.

I placed my hand over Reverend's, smiled, and turned to Douglas. "It's not one hundred percent, but I had my suspicions. I was going to tell you when we got home."

He was dumbstruck. Speechless. But the corner of his eyes welled with misty tears as he placed his hand on top of mine. Three hands energizing my womb. Goody Olson's voice played back to me: "*Three.*" Maybe this is what she meant?

"When did you? How did you?"

"I saw Goody Olson this morning, and she told me there is a high likelihood that..."

Douglas removed his hand and jammed his fists into his pockets. He eyed the Reverend coldly up and down. "You told Reverend Gentry before me?"

I gasped. "Heavens no!"

Reverend stepped back, removing his hand from my stomach. "Oh no, Douglas," he said. "She's *glowing*. Can't you see it?" He waved his hand in a circle in the space before me, the motion left behind sparkles like a candle flickering in the wind, and I was filled with a warmth on my insides, like taking a sip of rum and letting the spirit heat your blood from the belly up. Trails of light entranced me as I stared at his face from behind the circle. It was as if he created a mystical opening between us. Like fragments of stars flitting about in the air. I wanted to reach out and touch the circle, touch the stars, and pull the Reverend into the space with me.

With a quick jerk of his hand, the circle was gone. I looked at Douglas who was completely spellbound. His eyes were glazed over, his jaw slightly opened. It didn't look like Douglas—it was merely his shell. Like his life and person had been sucked into the circle and left behind his physical body.

I tapped his shoulder. "Douglas? Did you hear Reverend?"

"Glowing. Yes," he mumbled and slowly came back into himself. I darted my head around to see if anyone else in the congregation had witnessed what just happened, but it didn't seem so. All were wandering aimlessly, conversing, and drinking lemonade, with nary a clue as to what transpired.

A sharp scream rang out across the back lot, and we snapped our heads to locate the source of the sound. In the distance, closer to the back door of the church, a group of women huddled together in a circle. Their bodies hunched over, observing something hidden from my eye in the grass. The reverend took off at breakneck speed and parted the sea of women like Moses parting the sea. When they scattered enough to get a good view, I was able to see Winnie Gordon lying in the grass, surrounded by a pool of her own blood. Her bloodied dress and apron from the hips down looked like she had been mauled by some type of animal in the most sensitive of areas.

Suddenly, I remembered my vision. I used one hand to cover my body with my sweater and placed the other protectively on the book within the pocket of my apron.

Winnie cried out, and everyone was in a panic.

Chapter 4

"Get the wagon!"
"Take her to Goody Olson's!"
"How far along is she?"
"Was she feeling well today?"
"Did she fall?"
"What happened?"

And when it finally hit me what was happening, it was clear to see that Winnie had miscarried the baby. The evidence was plain as day. I had seen this happen one too many times with the women I had been close to—most memorably when my own mother lost the child she was supposed to have when Tansy was three and I was six. She had felt a sharp pain in her lower abdomen and doubled over at the kitchen table. I remember her tears and the blood—a thin line of water from the side of her eye and a thin line of red down the side of her thigh.

Shouts and screams rang in the evening air until finally Jedidiah and Reverend scooped Winnie up by her shoulders and ushered her to a wagon. Tansy insisted on accompanying them to show support for her lifelong, best friend in her moment of need. I cleared the congregation, telling everyone to go home and pray for Winnie and the unborn child. But something inside me knew a child was there no more. I replayed my visions against the reality of Winnie in the bloody grass, and an overwhelming feeling of guilt consumed me. Did I somehow foresee the expulsion of her womb? Did I predict it?

Did I cause it?

In my own personal panic, I also sent Douglas home. I told him I would help Reverend clean up while we waited for news about Winnie. I told him we would celebrate our good news in private as it was not proper to make a public announcement if Winnie had in fact lost a child. He understood and went on his way. But I was not so collected. My mind raced, and horrible, murderous visions invaded my mind. It was maddening, the amount of fear and guilt and anger I felt.

I made my way to the clearing in the Black Wood Forest in search of some type of solace. It was the only place I thought of where I knew I would be able to relax my thoughts and my body and my soul. My heart was heavy, so very, very heavy. I knelt on the cold ground and prayed to God to absolve me of any and all bad thoughts I had. I didn't do anything, yet I felt such a deep responsibility for all that blood...

Blodheksa.

The book throbbed against my thigh. I removed it from the apron and set it down on the ground in front of me, turning the pages furiously, looking for something that resembled answers or insight, but the language was one I could not understand, and I was overwhelmed and confused. Yet I was drawn to it, like it called my name amidst the cold night air, the pages running hot against my fingertips, the archaic letters humming in my ears. I finally turned to a page toward the back of the book, and there, in the language of my forefathers, was written, "Bloody seed between your legs."

Quickly, I slammed the book shut as a gush of wind howled in my face. Those were my words. Words spoken to pregnant Winnie Gordon just hours before she was no longer. My breath came in heavy gulps as I tried to wrestle with what was happening when, suddenly, movement from beyond the trees startled me to attention.

It was Reverend coming from the same direction I came. Did he follow me? Quickly, I reached for the book and slid it under my dress. He eyed it suspiciously as it slithered in the grass and disappeared under my knees, but he made no comment or question.

"Is this our special spot, or something?" He chuckled as approached me. "I figured I would find you here," he said, joining me on the ground. "You sister is worried about you."

"I'm fine," I said sharply.

"You're not. What perplexes you, Barbara?" He reached for my hand as I began to weep. "Are you sad about Winnie?"

I didn't respond. Because I was not. Deep down, I wasn't sad, and I thought I wept *because* I wasn't, not because I was, and that realization scared me.

"Father," I began, "I think I've done a terrible thing. I have to make a confession"

"What did I tell you about when we're alone together?" he reminded me.

"Galen," I corrected myself. "I apologize. Galen, I think I've done something terribly wrong."

"Of course, I will listen to your confession. What could you have possibly done?" he said, reassuring and in disbelief.

"I think what happened to Winnie Gordon is my fault," I confessed.

He squeezed my hands tighter together. "And what makes you think that?"

I breathed deeply and exhaled a white puff of frigid air. "I wished it," I said in a low, guilty voice.

Galen moved closer to me and wrapped his arm around my shoulder, bringing me into the crook of his arm. "It may seem like that, but..."

"I thought about it. Said the words. Hours later, it happened."

"Said the words?" he questioned.

I nodded.

"Speak of this to no one, Barbara."

"But you're my pastor. Are you refusing to absolve me of my sins?"

"There is no sin to be absolved from. You have done nothing wrong."

Angry, I moved from his embrace, revealing the book from under me. I didn't care. If he didn't believe me or take me seriously, I didn't care.

He picked it up and held it in front of him. "Blood Witch," he read before placing it back down on the ground. "Do you know why we call putting letters together to form words and sentences 'spelling'?"

I shook my head.

"Words have power, Barbara. Words can manifest into reality by the right people. Spoken words, written words, even words that take shape as visions in the mind's eye. Power. *Spells.* With the intention behind it, words can have an extreme amount of power to effect a change or result or something happening."

I scooped up the book, put it back in my pocket, and stood up at attention. I bounced from one leg to the next in a nervous and anxious way. "What are you saying?" I blurted frantically. "Am I in trouble? Did I really hurt Winnie's baby? Why won't you absolve me?" I cried again.

"I will not absolve you, Barbara," he said again. "I cannot absolve you. I told you there is nothing to absolve. You've done nothing wrong. Remember what I've said: 'do not speak of this to anyone else,' and 'your words have power.' That is all for now." He reached for my hands and held me at arms-length. A tingling sensation ran throughout my body and up to the top of my skull, like pinpricks poking and prodding at me. Like fingers trying to unfold pieces of my brain to look inside.

"I was there when it happened," he said, staring at my stomach.

I gasped and my face turned red with embarrassment.

He smiled at me—soothing and natural. The trees danced in his gray eyes and my shame melted away. A twitchy feeling swelled throughout my body and the wind blew in the space between us—not quite the circle of stars from earlier in the evening but magnetic energy spawning between us. I felt it in me, through me, around me, flowing from him. In a daze, he looked like a tall tree, gnarled and silver, with thick shady limbs. And in that moment, my heart fluttered and wanted to stay in the woods forever. "Is this a spell?" I asked dreamily.

"Oh, no, Barbara. There's no spell in the world that can bewitch you."

Chapter 5

Saturday, October 8th 1695
The Flynn Residence
New Haven Harbor, Massachusetts
Morning of the Night of the New Moon

I dreamed of Galen—often and on a consistent basis. Last night not being any exception either. Last night, we were in the clearing of the Black Wood Forest surrounded by black poplars and red roses. He spoke to me in a low voice, hypnotizing me. I wore a white nightgown that had brown splatter marks at the shoulders. My head itched. I reached my hand to feel the top of my head and was met by prickly thorns. "A crown for a queen," he said to me, but not with his mouth, not with his voice, not in this tongue—with the voice of a thousand stars, in a language I only knew deep in my soul. This dream was different from the others I had had of him—others where he and I were in the throes of passion doing unspeakable things. I lay in bed absorbing the memory of the dream and reflecting on the events of life as they played out before me.

While my newfound thoughts of motherhood filled most of my daily musings, when night fell, I was sure to see the bold chiseled face of my priest holder hovering over me in some wild and exotic fantasy. Shameful it was to continuously envision him as I tried to perform my wifely duties; pitiful it was to ignore the sweet and innocent advances from my doting husband in exchange for the savagery my brain concocted.

Poor Douglas was none the wiser. He had been walking with his head held high ever since I imparted the good news of my expectant nature to him. It was as if his entire demeanor had changed—no longer did he look at me with contempt or disappointment. Now he viewed me as a partner who had fulfilled both of our destinies. To say he was happy still wouldn't explain his excitement.

And as Douglas's happiness grew, *my* contempt and disappointment for *him* did as well. And I began to question the motives and intentions of our union. Was I only good enough for him now that I was with child? Even still, my lack of interest in anything involving him was becoming obvious. When he tried to engage me in conversation, I tuned him out. When he asked me anything about health or home, I responded with as few words as possible. When he coaxed me into lying with him at night, I could only stomach the act if I had someone else on my mind. And I was able to explain all that away by the fact that the child who was growing inside me was causing all kinds of changes within—nausea, mood swings, and general malaise—and that was sufficient for him. However, the part about my dreaming of Galen remained unbeknownst to Douglas.

But not to Galen.

Because somehow, someway, he *knew*. He knew I had thought about him the night my child was conceived. He knew I imagined being with him on a regular basis. And *he* knew that *I* knew that *he* knew. It was almost like a little game we played with each other. It started out with sideways glances as we passed each other by in the church or the brush of our hands as he bent down to help me refill the altar vases. One night, I dreamt of him in the form of a giant lion with a massive golden mane and strong muscles rippling against his taut, tawny frame. I was his lioness and knelt in submission to him as he mounted me and held me in place with his sharp teeth on the back of my neck. When I awoke, I could still hear the howls and roars from the two beasts. And later that afternoon, Galen had coincidentally quoted a Bible verse to Tansy and me: "Your adversary, the devil, prowls around like a roaring lion seeking someone to devour." But he stared straight at me with a knowing look that made my ears go hot with embarrassment.

It was as if he were inside my mind, beside me always. Like he could see through my closed eyes. No, more like he could tap into my third eye, not to control or manipulate me, but to watch, listen, and *observe*. Quickly, I shook my head to rid myself of such thoughts. Thoughts like those were works of the devil. There was a part of me—the part that was good, pure, and true—that hated to think those thoughts, wanted to be a good and faithful wife, longed to feel like a part of our community and family in faith, love, and happiness. But there was also a part of me—the part that was curious and full of wonder and awe—that loved my dreamy, nighttime visits, wanted to run away to the clearing and dance naked under the light of the full moon, and longed to decode the secrets of the *Blodheksa* book hidden underneath my garments.

A furious pounding on my front door broke me from the grip the devil had on my cognizance. Hurriedly, I got up from my bed, yelled, "One minute," and threw a shawl about my shoulders.

With a wild look of concern on her face and curly hair fraying at the sides from the undoing of her tight bun, Tansy's hazel eyes spoke volumes of her demeanor. "Get dressed!" she ordered. "Post haste!"

I ushered her in from the front steps and gently closed the door behind her. "What's wrong?" I asked. "What happened?"

"We need to get to the Meeting House. The Magistrate has called a town meeting."

"It's early! It's Saturday!" I exclaimed. "We have a few hours yet before we need to be at the church. And business isn't conducted on..."

"It is today!" she shouted, cutting me off.

I narrowed my eyes and placed my hands on my hips. "Temperance Wilkins," I said in my stern, older sister voice, "what are you not telling me?"

A wave of terror washed over her face, draining the color from her rosy cheeks. Pure fear in her eyes transformed her entire countenance. "You wouldn't believe me if I told you," she said solemnly.

We made our way to the Meeting House where the entire town had gathered. All present seemed to be huddled and whispering amongst themselves. At the front desk, Galen sat next to Magistrate John Williams. I caught his eye for a second, and he nodded his head to me in acknowledgment. Douglas was nowhere to be found, and I assumed he was unable to leave his post at the jail. The room was filled to the brim with bodies, and Tansy and I stood by the doors in the back.

The magistrate banged his gavel on the wooden desk, bringing us all to attention. "Everyone, everyone, settle down," he said in his deep voice as the gavel came down three more times in succession creating a hushed silence in the room. "I understand there are concerns over the events that transpired last night at the church, and we are here to collectively and calmly offer our eye-witness accounts and solutions."

I nudged Tansy on the arm. "What happened at the church?" I whispered.

Her gaze remained forward, and she bid me to be quiet.

"We'll begin with eyewitnesses. No hearsay or rumors, please. I wish to deal only in what was seen firsthand," the magistrate continued.

A woman in the front row raised her hand, and he called on her to speak. "It was awful!" she gushed. "Those poor little cats strewn all over the property."

"Goody Sheare, please elaborate. What business did you have? What exactly did you see?"

Goody Sheare stood up, approached the desk, and looked about the room. "I... I was going over to the church to deliver the reverend some food," she said sheepishly and clutched the sides of her shawl.

"At what hour was this?" the magistrate inquired.

"Before sunrise," she answered, and a questioning murmur rose from the audience. I looked at Tansy who raised her eyes back at me.

"I... I... I guess I wasn't paying too much attention to the time. I had made some bread and churned some butter the previous day and decided to bring it over with some fresh fruit. I... I just didn't pay attention." Her voice trailed, and the audience chattered.

"Since Martin passed, she *has* been a little out of sorts," Tansy said from the corner of her mouth.

Still, I thought, such odd behavior for a newly widowed woman in her thirties. Apparently, the rest of the town thought so too.

"I don't sleep well these days," she continued. "I often find myself cooking or sewing at all times of the day."

"And stargazing," someone in the hall muttered under their breath with an accusatory tone.

Magistrate Williams heaved the gavel again and when the crowd quieted, he continued, getting back to the issue at hand, "Goody Sheare, what did you see upon approaching the church?"

She made a little hitch in her throat and gave two quick coughs. "It was the worst thing I've ever seen!"

"Embellish," I whispered playfully to Tansy, but she did not return a glance or smile or even an arm-swat.

"Cats. Hundreds of them. Torn to pieces like some wild thing had gotten to them and massacred in chaos. So much blood in the grass." Her eyes glazed over with the memory of the scene.

"A coyote? Or a bobcat?" one of the men offered as an explanation.

"No," she replied, still half in her trance. "They were mutilated. On purpose. No animal is capable of the sadistic and ritualistic way in which they were... were... *sacrificed.*"

A panicked din swelled in the room, and the magistrate banged his gavel again. "Alright! Alright!" he boomed, but it was obvious he struggled to maintain order.

Mr. Jensen raised his hand and stood up. "If this is what Goody Sheare says it is—a sacrifice—are we heading into Salem territory?"

Another tense shift blanketed the room.

"Who could have done this?"

"What about the missing children in Salem? They were playing in the gallows, and..."

"Let's make a list of where everyone was so that we can narrow it down!"

"I was asleep; my wife can vouch for that."

"Who worked an overnight shift? Who was at the jail?"

"Are we under attack?"

"We should form a watch group."

My heart sank for a second at the rising unease.

Magistrate looked to Galen for help with the barrage of questions, and Galen raised his hand before he spoke. "Let's not assume the worst. It's probably just a prank. A very twisted and bizarre prank, but a prank all the same. There's been nearly three years of peace and silence, and I don't see why that would have to stop now. Let's allow Salem, and all of Massachusetts, time to heal. The last thing is to get into a panic. We need to learn from their mistakes and have the foresight not to repeat them. What happened on the lawn is reprehensible, but I will show mercy and forgiveness to those individuals who had a moment of weakness and strayed to the side of the devil. If that person or persons has the true essence of sorrow and regret in their heart, they will be absolved. We must all show compassion and forgiveness, for it is God's will. New Haven Harbor is a good place, a pure place, a place of sanctity and love. We will not let one act of wickedness cloud our judgement. We will not let one act of mischief snuff out the light of our town."

Magistrate smiled, for Galen had said the words that he never could. A sigh of calm temporarily fell over the crowd.

"And remember," Galen continued, "keep your good thoughts flowing..."

"And your actions to match," the congregation said in unison.

The Magistrate banged his gavel one final time, dismissing the group.

From across the room, Galen caught my eye and nodded to me again. I remembered what he told me the other night about words having power, and I knew the spell he cast on the crowd would only placate them for so long.

Tansy and I left and headed over to the church for work. A crowd had already begun gathering around by the time we arrived. Swarms of people hovered along the fence, menfolk on the lawn pitched in to clear the area of the gruesome scene, and a line of townswomen with plates of food anxiously awaited the arrival of the reverend. I slowed my pace to spy the horror on the lawn. The sight was curiously familiar to me—the way the animals were aligned and arranged reminded me of the evening Tansy and I came upon the tableau in the clearing. And the way the blood of the dead cats stained the thinning autumn grass a deep shade of brown reminded me of when the blood poured from Winnie's womb. My head felt unclear as I strolled along, like a slow burning throb of a headache. I chalked it up to the unborn child within me making its presence known and felt, and I continued to the front door of the church where the townswomen waited for Reverend to open the doors. It burned me inside to see them fawn all over him—the way they giggled and batted their eyes, the way they positioned their braids over one shoulder, the way they swished their skirts to and fro. "Oh, Reverend!" they would gush and playfully hold tight to his upper arm with laughter. Old Man Boone was dead and buried, and long from everyone's memory, because the moment Galen Gentry came to town, it seemed the women flocked to every sermon, every service, and every village green event.

And it burns me.

Standing first in line at the church door, Winnie Gordon held a massive plate covered with a checkered print cloth. I heard her boast loudly to Margaret Fletcher (who stood in line behind her) that she had whipped up some of her famous hasty pudding and corn bread because Reverend had told her it was his favorite. My stomach turned upon hearing those lies, and I realized that both Winnie and Goody Fletcher were not at the Meeting Hall and had probably been standing here at the church doors all morning.

The door eventually opened, and Galen heartily greeted the throng, but he did not let any enter. He craned his neck and scanned the crowd, and when our eyes met, he waved me in. I grabbed Tansy's hand and pushed through the crowd of women, purposefully bumping their hips and knocking into their home cooked delights. Winnie crinkled her nose as I marched past her, but I ignored it and smiled gaily at Galen. I headed straight to the altar to change out the flowers, but listened intently as the women barreled in. Tansy remained by Galen's side to receive their gifts.

Later, most of the crowd had dispersed back to their normal lives. Tansy and I finished our daily duties, and I sent Tansy home. The men had finished with the removal and disposal of the horror scene, and the women had finished doting over the good Reverend.

All except Winnie.

I was collecting the candles in the vestibule when I saw her approach Galen at the altar. He was reading scripture, preparing for the Sunday service, when she tugged on his coat sleeve until he looked up at her. "Oh, Reverend!" she said dramatically. "I really can't thank you enough for all the guidance and support you've given me in my time of need."

"Don't mention it, my dear." He smiled. "No woman should have to experience what you did. But the Lord works in mysterious ways. And your faith is strong."

"Oh yes! It is, Father. And because of you, my faith has been restored seven-fold. I have re-dedicated myself to my faith and my church." She ran her hand down the side of his arm in a suggestive manner, one that was too familiar for a priest and his subject. "I am willing to serve," she purred.

He licked his lips, and I stopped what I was doing to focus my attention on them. The air about them turned fuzzy, and it was hard for me to see clearly. Galen motioned his hand in front of her and there were stars again. Twinkling stars in a circle swirling in the space between them. I was now an outsider looking in. *Looking through.* Reality had shifted into a foggy haze. Suddenly, he grabbed her shoulders, hoisted her onto the edge of his altar, and lifted her pinafore to expose the lower half of her body. Her golden sex glistened and reflected off the marble top giving her the illusion of having two private regions. One lady part real, the other some magic trick or mirage. *Double the pleasure.* He undid the buckle of his belt and let his britches fall to the floor. His raging manhood sprang out from underneath his long shirt, and he quickly entered her, plunging wildly as she moaned.

I was angry. Dumbstruck. Jealous. All those negative and forbidden feelings attributed to this negative and forbidden act. For Galen had ravaged me every night in my dreams, and here he was, committing the act with Winnie Gordon in the most blasphemous of ways. For some reason, I counted. I counted every thrust, every stab-like motion.

One. Two. Three. Four. Five. Six. Seven.

You restored my faith seven-fold, her words came back to me.

She arched her back and gave out a cry. Her body shook. That's when I saw the font of blood spurt from between her legs and onto the altar floor. And as his manhood released, it was not the fleshy organ riddled with veins like I had imagined it to be, but it was a knife, bloodied to the hilt. I blinked rapidly to clear my eyes, to rid myself of the sacrilegious scene, but in an instant, it was over. Galen waved his hand again, and the stars disappeared. The world looked clear and crisp, like nothing had ever transformed. Winnie stood next to him, her hand gripping his arm, and her eyes closed. I knew she too had seen the same thing, felt it, experienced it. She opened her eyes and her cheeks flushed hot, but he tilted his head with a puzzled expression.

"Are you feeling well, Winifred?" he asked gently.

"Oh... um... yes, yes..." she stammered, flustered. A jolt of dread overcame her as the blood quickly drained from her face. She went from rose red to stark white in seconds.

"Do you wish for me to escort you home?"

"No... no... I'm... I'm fine. Just lost track of time. I'll be going now." She smoothed her hands down the front of her pinafore, as if she were mentally checking that it hadn't been disturbed. "Good evening, Reverend," she said and hurriedly scurried out of the church.

I soon understood that what I saw was merely an illusion, and the jealous fire that had smoldered in my heart quickly started to fade.

Galen turned his head in my direction and raised his eyebrows, beckoning me to comment on what transpired.

"That was a show?" I asked. "A trick?"

"Something like that."

"What did you show her?"

He smiled wide, showing me the rows of his devilishly white teeth, knowing full well I knew the answer to my question. "I showed her only what she wanted to see."

"Then, why did you show it to me?" I countered.

"Because you wanted to see it too."

"No, I didn't," I blurted.

He paused, breathed in loudly, and exhaled. "You're right. You didn't want to *see* it."

Why would I want to see that when it happens to me every night in my dreams? I said to myself on the inside, for I didn't want him to hear my words.

"True," he responded, and I knew he had read my thoughts.

"You'll show me?" I inquired.

"When you're ready."

"And when will I be ready?"

"Soon."

Chapter 6

Saturday, October 22nd 1695
New Haven First Church of God
The Nuptials of Temperance Wilkins and John Foster
New Haven Harbor, Massachusetts
The Night of the Full Moon

My time spent at the church grew more and more with each passing day, just like the little life growing inside me. The reality of the child's presence was made fully aware when I did not bleed at the appropriate time, but Goody Olson had said I would undergo a proper examination by the end of the next moon cycle. In the meantime, she gave me an herbal tea to drink a few times a week to help with any morning illness I felt and to put me in what she called a "calming state." So, I spent my days with two things in mind: serving Galen and the church and nurturing the life growing inside me.

One night, I had arrived home from the church later than usual. Dinner had not yet been prepared, and Douglas sat in the parlor with a rather cross face. When he questioned me about my whereabouts, I was quick to remind him that my service was payment for our prayers being answered. What an auspicious time for Reverend Gentry to have taken over the priesthood at the same time of our conception. After all our prayers! After all our wanting and pleading with God! It was my duty to be at Reverend's beck and call to show our deepest gratitude for the answering of our petition.

"But it wasn't the Reverend who answered our prayers, Barbara," he had snapped and jumped from the chair.

"It very well could have been!" I snapped back. "Reverend Gentry is an agent of the Lord. It is through him that all works are done."

Douglas threw his hands in the air and huffed. "He's just a man!"

"Just a man? With the power to forgive the sins of the people. If he has that power alone—to lift our transgressions up to the Lord with his holy voice and bring forth to us the most holy of absolutions—then what is he, if not imbued with the agency of God?"

He could no longer argue with me. He scratched his head and paced the wooden floor. His heavy soles shuffled along the planks, and the mere sound of it made me wince with disgust. Without haste, I prepared his supper and gave myself to him that night like the good wife I was, for I was not about to further the topic or have him interrogate me again. I feared that if Douglas pried any deeper into my heart and mind, or even into the hat box at the back of my closet, there would be very many other questions for me to defend against. And who knew what repercussions would wait for me if that were to happen? Wrapped in a silken handkerchief that had been passed to me from my grandmother Abigail Wilkins, the forbidden book with the title *Blodheksa, Blodbrødre, og Blodsøster* was hidden nicely in a box in the darkest part of my closet. Thankfully, long ago, I had stressed to Douglas the importance of a woman's privacy in the areas of hygiene and dress, and he had respected those demands. I had heard stories of the other women whose husbands were brutish and demanded to know every aspect of their wives' personal life, so I considered myself lucky in that regard.

Whenever I could steal away, I visited with the book. I sifted through the pages, tried pronouncing the foreign words, and tried feeling the energy that emitted from them. I knew not what the words meant, but I *did*. They sang to me. I heard them—not in my conscious mind of the English language, but something deeper—a primordial song that only I could hear, that only I could feel, that only I could *know*.

There was no doubt the book was an ancient tome. Its yellowed pages were crisp and frayed at the edges. I knew it had seen many a year and many a handler, and when I ran my fingers across the unfamiliar text, I envisioned a golden-haired woman with long straggly braids handing a battle axe to her lover and saying the words from the book to wrap him in a white protective light. I envisioned a young black-haired woman singing in the woods at night, her hands enveloped around a man's throat to conjure the most arcane magic to do her bidding. I envisioned a silver-haired crone with a black robe draped about her shoulders. Her outstretched arms bore carvings of archaic symbols, and her wrists dripped with blood. She said the words from the book as a little boy stood in awe before her.

A little boy with the face of Galen Gentry.

It was wrong—so very, very wrong—having the book in my possession, reading from it (although I knew not the words), longing to spend time with it—I knew it. I knew the dark magics that resided deep in the book had been burrowing their way into my very being. I knew if I had been caught or had mentioned any of this to anyone, the curse of Salem would rain down upon me.

But it felt good. Warm. Soothing. Like the way too much rum made your head feel fuzzy. My father had always said that anything that felt too good was a gift from the devil, and for that, I felt a slight shame. My father's disappointment would bring me great sadness, but I was too entranced to stop. Mystified. Every time I cradled the book between my two palms, a rush came over me— like an extra breath breathed into my lungs, giving me a weightless and euphoric feeling. And

Chapter 6

like the child in my womb, my curiosity grew. It knew no bounds.

I had almost lost track of time when I heard Douglas bounding up the steps. I hurriedly packed my special book away into its secret space by the time he reached the bedroom door.

Knelt over, I turned my head when he walked in and smiled.

"Are you alright?" he asked.

"Yes, yes. Thought I had a different pair of shoes but can't find them. I can't remember if I gave them to the donation box or not," I lied so easily.

"Well, enough with that fussing. You don't want to be late for your sister's wedding day, do you?"

I rose and smoothed out the front of my dress.

"Heavens, no!" I exclaimed with a forced laugh, and we made our last rounds of the house and headed to the church.

It was an important day for the Wilkins family. Their youngest daughter, and last child, was to be married to a respected man. My parents beamed with pride and joy at the thought of their baby girl going off into the world on her own and becoming her own person. I'm sure the thought of having their own freedom back was nice too. And though they were happy and proud, I know it bothered my father something awful that the Wilkins name would no longer carry on. My oldest brother, John, had succumbed to yellow fever, leaving his young wife a widow before they could procreate. My second oldest brother,

Thomas, had been killed in a hunting accident before he was of age to marry. My third oldest brother, William, had no interest in the company of women and sought adventure out west. He left with a party on his sixteenth birthday and hadn't been heard from since. After Tansy, mother miscarried a fourth boy, all unfortunate events befalling the men of the house which further perpetuated the idea in father's mind that the Wilkins family was cursed.

The responsibility of carrying the Wilkins' blood lay solely on Tansy and my shoulders. Up until most recently, my parents had thought it would be up to only Tansy. But even still, our children would be Flynns and Fosters, and while my mother was ecstatic at the prospect of cherubic grandchildren, my father would always look at them as slightly ... less.

Douglas took his seat next to my parents in the front pew on the right-hand side of the church. Mother and Father greeted him with hearty smiles and warm regards. The left side of the church was already packed with Fosters from all over. Mother looked around and gave a meek smile. I knew it must have broken her heart to think of her lost boys not being able to celebrate their sister's special day. It must have broken her heart twice over to see the lack of family support for her daughter and to have to host all these strangers turned kin at her home immediately following. But how can you have family support when there is barely a family?

"Fosters galore!" I remarked to her. "I bet half of them aren't even related!"

Mother smiled a closed-lipped smile; Father grunted something unintelligible.

"Is the house prepared?" I asked.

Mother nodded. "The cakes are set on the table, and the spirits are ready to be poured," she replied, trying to maintain an air of excitement.

"Alright," I squeezed her hand. "I'll go to the back to check on Tansy."

Tansy stood in front of the large mirror in the back room swishing her hips to and fro, admiring the way her body fit against her ivory dress. I clapped my hands in delight, and she stopped, startled, and grinned at me. "Is it acceptable?" she asked nervously.

"Better than acceptable," I gushed.

"Will John like it?"

"Oh sweetheart, John will like anything he sees you in!"

She blushed. "Is everyone here? Is it almost time?"

"The Fosters are practically spilling from out the front door. I'd say there are plenty. Our side? Well, you knew what to expect with that."

She gave a small grimace.

"I think we're just waiting on your dear friend, Winnie, and her most esteemed husband…" I said with sarcasm but stopped when Tansy's face melted into a look of despair.

"Winnie's not coming," she said tersely.

"Not coming?"

"No, Barbara, she's not. She, nor Jedidiah."

"Is she ill? Is she alright? I don't understand why she would miss the most special day of her best friend!" My voice rose with anger, and my hatred for the woman surfaced on my tongue.

Tansy wrung her hands together and meticulously cracked each individual knuckle of each individual finger.

"Stop that!" I admonished.

"Oh. Sorry, sorry!" she apologized, as if she had been unaware of her actions in the first place.

"Well, did she tell you why she wasn't coming?" I pressed.

"Yes," she began. "She's sick. Sick at heart."

"Sick at heart? What do you mean, 'sick at heart?'"

"I... I don't know if I should say..." she stammered. "I promised Winnie I wouldn't..."

My blood boiled at the thought of my sister keeping secrets from me, and a thin veil of red descended in front of my eyes. "Promised Winnie what? You know I tell you everything!" I cried out, but as the words flew from my lips, I knew they were lies for I had been hiding much, and more, these days from my darling sister.

Tansy paused. Hesitated.

"I'll tickle it out of you!" I said playfully, trying to lighten the mood.

She gave a soft smile. "I don't know," she repeated.

I placed my hands on my hips in a defiant stance. "What? You can't trust me now?"

Her hazel eyes went wide. "Oh no! That's certainly not it! It's just that... that... you're so close to the reverend, and..."

"Winnie's sick at heart because of Reverend?" I said in a disbelieving tone.

"She told me things..."

"What *things*?" I demanded.

"She said she doesn't feel right around him. He gives her a weird feeling. She hasn't been to service in weeks now because of it."

I hadn't even noticed Winnie's absence from church. "Did she tell you why? Specifically?"

"No. Nothing specific, per se. Just that whenever she's around him, she feels... fuzzy. Bewitched."

I tensed up at attention but lowered my voice to a whisper. "Did she use that exact word? *Bewitched*?"

Tansy nodded quickly.

"Tansy Wilkins, it would do you a world of good to never repeat that again! Especially with the use of that particular word!" I scolded. "Don't even dare utter that nasty rumor to anyone. You know Winnie just lost a child. That had to have been a traumatic experience for her. Who knows what that did to her mind? I remember how Mother became a little touched after she lost her last boy in the womb. And to think, Winnie lost the baby on church grounds! Maybe she's equating the reverend with the bad feelings and memories she has of that moment. She just needs time to heal."

"I suppose you're right," she relented. "And that's probably the last time you'll ever be able to call me that again."

My face twisted with mild confusion. "Tansy Wilkins?"

"I'll be Goody Foster in no time!" She beamed.

I suddenly snapped back into the now and then. "Oh, good gracious! We should be on our way! You're to be a wife ten minutes ago!" She grabbed my hands lovingly and we both laughed. I quickly shuffled back to my lonely family at the first pew, and Tansy exited the back to make her grand entrance from the front doors.

The glow of dusk-time radiated around her as she and my father walked slowly down the aisle. The Foster-folk 'ooohh'ed and 'aaahh'ed as she strode past them. John Foster and the reverend waited for her at the altar. My father kissed her clasped hands, presented them to John, and sat down next to my mother. Douglas squeezed the top of my knee, probably in a moment of nostalgia. I placed my hand lovingly on top of his as the ceremony began.

Reverend stood in the middle of John and Tansy with his outstretched arms, much like the silver-haired crone from my vision. I shuddered with sadness on the inside—the thought of my precious book tucked silently away made my heart hurt for a second.

"Dearly beloved," Galen addressed us, "we are gathered here in the sight of God, and in the face of this Congregation, to join together this Man and this Woman in holy Matrimony..."

John Foster's mother clutched her chest with pride. Some of the Foster women sighed. Tansy looked to John, the light of love and God exuded all around her, enveloping them both in a dream-like swirl. Their love was palpable, and all knew this was the happiest day of both of their lives.

Reverend looked directly at me. His mouth moved with some more of the wedding ceremony vows, but I could not hear them. I was swept away in his eyes—the gray forest with woodland creatures scampering about. And in the woodland forest, the Black Wood, I saw two figures standing naked, face to face, much like John and Tansy were at the altar. Only it wasn't John and Tansy, and it wasn't the church. The naked couple held hands in a circle of twigs. A silver light shone down from the treetops. The silver light of the full moon. I quivered and removed my hand from the top of Douglas's.

"Wilt thou, Temperance Wilkins, have this man, John Foster the third, to thy wedded husband, to live together after God's ordinance, in the holy estate of matrimony? Wilt thou obey him, serve him, love, honor, and keep him in sickness and in health, and forsaking all others, keep thee only unto him, so long as ye both shall live?"

But Galen spoke to *me*. He spoke the words deep in my heart, deep in the woods. His mouth moved in his eyes and the song rang out across the clearing: *Wilt thou, Barbara Flynn, have this man,*

Galen Gentry? The words were strange to my ears, but the message held true. I heard it. I felt it. I wanted it and needed it.

"I will," I whispered in the woods.

"I will," Tansy replied proudly to the church.

"John Foster," Galen continued, "repeat these sacred words after me to seal the vow that you do so profess in front of kin on this twenty-second day of October, year of our Lord, sixteen hundred and ninety-five: With this Ring, I thee wed, with my body, I thee worship, and with all my worldly goods, I thee endow."

John took out a ring from his pocket, placed it on Tansy's finger, and repeated the words.

But Galen spoke to *me* again, there in the woods, but there was no token, no symbol, no physical ring to solidify our union. Instead, he moved his arm about in a semi-circle and engulfed us in a swirling ring of stars as if the universe itself had blessed us directly.

"By the powers vested in me from the Lord on High, I, Reverend Galen Gentry, now pronounce you man and wife. You may now kiss your bride."

John swept Tansy close to him at the waist and planted a glorious open-mouth kiss on his new wife as the congregation exploded in applause. I wriggled away from Douglas's touch as inconspicuously as I could.

And as the voices around me cheered for the newlywed couple as they exited the building, I remained in the clearing. Galen did the same as John had done to Tansy — pulled me close at

the waist, ran his hand up my bare back creating hen-flesh throughout, and kissed me hard.
His tongue darted in and out of my mouth as
our lips opened and closed, opened, and closed.
The passion burned deep in me, and his organ
throbbed at my leg. And unlike Tansy and John,
I was soon underneath Galen in the grass where
we kissed wildly and passionately until he eased
my legs apart and entered me to consummate our
unholy union.

Chapter 7

Monday, October 31st 1695
New Haven First Church of God
All Hallow's Eve
New Haven Harbor, Massachusetts
The First Night of the Waning Crescent Moon

From 1689 through 1692, two-hundred people were officially accused of practicing the dark arts in Salem. Thirty of them were found guilty. Nineteen were hanged. Five died while incarcerated. Two babies were born in jail cells. And it all started when eleven-year-old Abigail Williams and nine-year-old Betty Parris were having a joke. A game. Fits of madness, perhaps. Lies, most likely. And Tituba, the caretaker from foreign lands, would forever be regarded as some Voodoo Queen, some evil-mastermind witch with a secret book and spells for days. By the time the affliction had spread throughout their village and started to infect the neighboring towns, the jokes and lies had manifested into something beyond anyone's control. It was madness, driven by madness, driven by fear and anxiety, and a need to control what could not be seen. For a while, it seemed as if anyone could point a gnarled finger at anyone else and lunacy ensued.

Reverend Boone had been our wise advisor during those years and had kept his flock of sheep safe from the sickness. He harbored the people of New Haven Harbor to not let us fall prey to the Folly. Whatever magic was bestowed upon him was enough to get us through the three years of the insanity surrounding us. Which is not to say the townspeople didn't talk—because we were the worst offenders. Which is not to say the townspeople weren't curious—because we were. Which is not to say the townspeople didn't seek out stories and mischief of our own—because we did. But our gossip and musings were a far cry from the gallows over in Salem with bodies swaying in the wind.

So old business is old business and new business is new business, and while still a fresh wound, the infection in Salem had healed, Reverend Boone was long gone, and I had borne witness to ungodly, otherworldly sights. I wondered if Tituba was the genuine article after all. I knew what tortures she endured for just speaking the name of the *Malleus Maleficarum*. What would they do to me if my possession of the *Blodheksa* book had been revealed? What would become of me if my secret spiritual wedding to our pastor became known? What trials and tribulations would *I* suffer? *Thou shalt not suffer a witch to live.* I feared the fibers of our tightly knit community had become threadbare. Or maybe it was just me—unraveling. Becoming undone—becoming undone and *becoming*, again.

The All Hallow's Eve feast took place on the lawn of the church. Unlike most other villages that celebrated their festivals at their designated meeting houses or village greens, New Haven Harbor used the First Church of God for mostly all our communal events. And in accordance with the laws and traditions, the celebration was one of reverence and little merriment. Much to the displeasure of the older generation, some of the children had carved out turnips, lit candles in them, and decorated the back porch of the church. Some played games, and the bigger ones told ghost stories to the younger ones in hurried whispers at each corner of the field. When the sun had set, the cider was gone, and the bitter cold wind hurt the edges of our ears, the crowd dispersed, and Tansy and I set out to tidy up the last of the festivities.

Goody Olson had lingered in the yard whence everyone had gone. Her back hunched forward slightly as if to keep her body warm. She hobbled over to us with slow and deliberate movements and her dark green cloak dragged behind her. "Dear child!" she called, and her voice wavered in the wind.

"Goody Olson!" I exclaimed in surprise. "Whatever are you doing? You should be home by now." Quickly, I attended to her and threw an arm around her shoulder. Tansy stood a short distance from us, observing with a watchful eye.

Chapter 7

"I almost forgot, child," Goody said and pulled out a capped mug from the depth of her cloak. "Your drink."

"It's Monday?" I inquired. "Oh, heavens! It is, isn't it? I nearly forgot. I was so preoccupied with..."

Goody smiled wide and the wrinkles around her eyes crinkled together like deep valleys racing across her face. "I know, I know," she said handing me the cup. "Now drink up before the night is done."

I took the mug from her, lifted the cap, and swallowed deep. Goody's eyes twinkled and she nodded. "There, there. I'll be seeing you soon."

"G'night, Goody," I said.

"G'night." She craned her neck so she could better see Tansy in the yard. "G'night, Temperance Foster!" she called. "I hope to be seeing you soon as well!"

"Oh, yes," Tansy replied with a wave, "that seems to be the plan."

Goody nodded at me one last time, and I watched as she made her way to the front of the church. When she was out of earshot, Tansy raced over to me with a worried expression.

"Come inside, Barbara," she commanded, "it's getting colder out here."

"It is? I hadn't even noticed."

"What was in that drink she gave you?"

"What?"

Tansy's body tensed. "The drink. From Goody Olson. What is it?"

87

My face twisted in confusion. "You know what it is. It's the herbal tea for expectants."

"What does it taste like?"

I ran my tongue across the roof of my mouth to try to savor the last remnants of the concoction. "Hmmm," I mused, "herbs, some jasmine, definitely honey. Bitter, but sweet, if that makes sense. And a little smoky. I don't know. I can't really explain the flavor. It's robust. Unlike any normal drink, if that's what you mean."

"Does it taste like medicine?"

"Not necessarily. Not like the brews you drink when you're sick, but there is definitely a medicinal air to it."

"Does it taste like … poison?"

"Poison?" I bellowed in shock. "Why ever would you say that?"

She ignored my query and continued, "But what *is* it? Why do you drink it?"

"Because it helps with the sickness that befalls a woman in my condition. Goody says as the baby grows, it drains the mother. The drink calms us, rejuvenates us. A natural remedy for our nerves, soul, blood, and spirit. It helps to ease the pain and discomfort of our changing bodies. Why all the inquiries, sweet sister? Are you nervous for when it is your turn?"

"No," she spat and looked to the ground.

My ears piqued with interest at her abrupt response. "Oh? What then?"

Her feet shuffled underneath her, crunching the dead leaves at her soles. "It's just that..." her voice trailed.

"What?" I pressed.

"It's just that Winnie says Goody gave her a similar drink—jasmine. But Winnie told Goody she had no pain or discomfort and that everything was fine. Winnie was quite familiar with the changes of her body as it was not her first time with child you know. She didn't want the drink, but Goody insisted anyway, and surmising Goody knew what she was talking about..."

"Goody Olson *does* know what she's talking about!" I defended.

"Well, Winnie didn't feel right about it, and look what tragedy befell her."

I narrowed my eyes in disgust. "Are you saying that Goody Olson purposefully *did* something to Winnie?"

Her lips smacked together with a tiny popping sound, and she tilted her head forward to come close to whisper in my ear. "Winnie says Goody Olson is a witch."

I pulled back in shock at her ominous words, my head snapping at attention. My anger rose to the base of my skull and filled my ears with a throbbing sensation. I looked to the sides of us in the yard to see if we were alone. I shuddered to think if anyone had heard such a dangerous accusation. "Hush your mouth, Tansy Foster! Say no more! Say no such thing again! Goody Olson has prepared herbs and spices and drinks for expectant mothers her entire life. I don't give a care what Winnie Gordon says or thinks. Can't you see she is still despondent over what happened to her? She's always been a hateful, jealous woman, and now she can add on 'sad' as well. All of that combined makes for an ill-omened situation."

"I just worry for you," she said meekly.

I breathed deeply to steady myself. "And yourself as well, I understand." I exhaled sharply, the white wind blowing about Tansy's pale face. "Your friendship with Winnie is precious to you, I understand. You take what she says as valued advice, I understand. But tread carefully. For your words have power, Tansy." Galen's voice broke into my mind, guiding me, calling to me. I paused and inhaled again. "And words with power can create something you're not ready to endure. Go home to John. Pray. Rest. Give your worries up to the Lord. Tomorrow is another day."

She nodded and side-stepped past me, but she never looked me in the eyes. Hers were still fixed on the wintery ground. I hoped for my sake and the sake of all New Haven Harbor that Tansy would heed my admonition and forsake those thoughts of witchery and allegations, but I knew deep down she would not.

Without warning, a piercing pain stabbed me in the abdomen, and I doubled over slightly from the sensation. *Mustn't get too worked up*, I thought to myself, and I remained motionless until the ache subsided. When it did, I began to walk back into the church to close out for the night and bid farewell to Galen, but within four steps or so, the agony took over again and dropped me to my knees.

I cried out in terror to the night sky, and in an instant, Galen was by my side. He put his shoulder underneath the crook of my arm and brought me to my feet. I was able to take a few steps before the sting rocked my insides again. Without hesitation, he swept me up into his arms and carried me to his chambers.

"What's wrong? What happened?" he asked as he laid me down on his bed.

My head swam, and my vision was blurry. Was I going in and out of the conscious world? Quite possibly so. The dull ache stemming from my womb grew more intense, more pronounced, and I struggled with the words to explain what happened. "I... I don't know. I was with Tansy and drank my drink. Tansy and I had some words, and..." My head rolled to the side. "It hurts," I said, grimacing.

"Where?" he asked gently.

"The baby," I answered. A warm gush of wetness released from between my legs. I reached my hand to inspect, and when I pulled them up, my fingertips were stained with a bright red secretion.

Blood.

"I'm losing the baby!" I screamed frantically.

"Oh no, Barbara," he said with calming concern. "Just relax. I'm right here with you. I will help you through this."

Tears streamed down my cheeks. "I can't lose my baby! My sweet, sweet baby!" It was becoming harder and harder to catch my breath. Thoughts of Winnie screaming in the bloody grass, thoughts of my mother moping in despondency, thoughts of Douglas's accusatory face when I told him the child was gone—it all rushed to me at once and made my heart beat so frenetically I was convinced it would beat out of my chest. I remembered Tansy's warning of Goody Olson, and fear struck me deep. Was it true? Was Goody Olson plotting something so nefarious that both Winnie Gordon and I miscarried our children so close together? How many other families had she ripped apart from the womb? "Goody Olson!" I exclaimed. "Tansy warned me of the drink!"

Galen grabbed at my hand with the bloodied fingers and wiped it away in his own before clutching them again. He gazed deeply into my eyes and smiled. "No, no, sweet lady. Goody Olson bears no ill-will."

I peered back into the gray storm of his eyes, and my heart quickly slowed tremendously to a more normal rhythm.

"You are going to lose the baby, Barbara. You cannot stop it. The waning moon wills for it so."

"But, why?" I pleaded, hoping he would have the magical answer.

He squeezed my hand tight. "Because you have to," he coaxed, and his eyes drifted upward to the ceiling.

I followed his gaze, and to my surprise, there was no ceiling above us. The stone had been replaced with sky—a marvelous night sky with the outline of the newly waning moon and a million stars. I blinked my eyes to get a better look at the wonder, and I gasped—gasped from a bout of pain and the sight of the beauty.

My womb contracted with spasm after spasm, but I remained focused on the sky. It was as if the stars breathed and pulsed in time with each constriction of my insides, for each time the throbbing pain pushed its way out of me, I noticed a disturbance, much like a torn piece of material, getting larger and wider, ripping open the sky to reveal the very essence of time and space. I was entranced. Mesmerized. I felt myself floating up to the opening among the stars, although I knew I was rooted in reality on Galen's bed. But I got closer and closer and reached out my hand to see what was beyond. The colored light coming from the gap sparkled. Twinkled. Danced. The light danced with life as I excreted what once was life inside me. I no longer cared about the blood between my legs for when I pushed a hand through the rip in the sky, the light illuminated my face and my soul with a million stars. I knew it to be *Time*. The great expanse of the universe. It was the face of God and all his angels and demons and devils. It was the face of the unholy beast called Satan. It was the beginning and end of all things. Alpha and Omega. I looked down to the bed, no longer in my body. The energy of the purest degree pulled me. Sucked me. Beckoned me to be one with it. There was peace in the opening. There was pleasure in the gash, like the pleasure a man feels when he enters a woman's body and becomes one with her. And there was chaos. And anarchy. And mischief. The Light was absolute as it gnashed the tail of the Darkness. The Darkness was absolute as it snuffed out the life of the Light. I longed to be one with it. Longed to stay within the source of all things and be one with the energy. I felt no pain.

"It's so… so… beautiful," I moaned, transfixed on the transcendent portal before me.

"What do you see?" Galen whispered in my ear, but his voice was an echo across the cosmos.

"Everything."

"Where are you?" he asked.

"Everywhere."

He kissed me gently on my forehead and said, "Come back to me."

With one last contraction, I drifted back into myself, back to the bloodied bed of my lost child. I looked about the room and wept, for the sorrow of the loss and the longing for eternity quickly manifested its way deep into my soul.

"I don't understand." I cried profound sobs that heaved my chest up and down.

"But you do, Barbara. You do." His voice wasn't his voice. It was deep and guttural, like a low beating drum singing in the winter night. And his words weren't his words, but the symbols on the pages of *Blodheksa*—ancient ruins given human tongue.

His face was blurred by my tears, but I could still decipher his countenance. Behind the mist, I saw past his disguise—a twisted mass of space and time that frightened me for but a second. I blinked to clear the tears, and Galen's human visage morphed back to me.

"Your womb is clean now. You can now bear the fruit of the Red Thorn."

I closed my eyes, my spirit still adjusting to the return to my body. "But Douglas. What shall I tell him?" The words sounded desperate even to my own ears.

"Nothing. It is done. You will be but a month off, but the Blood Brother and Blood Sister's arrival will not need the full amount of gestation, for they will not be ordinary children."

I tried to understand him, but my mind was not making rational connections with his words.

He smoothed my hair back from my face. "Remember what I told you about spells?'

I nodded.

"You transcended, my dear. There is a power inside you that will not and cannot be suppressed or contained, but it must be honed, nurtured, perfected. I've known you from the earliest spring of life, sought you out from across the sea, followed you through the breath of time. And you've known it too. Felt it. Felt my eyes watching from afar, heard my voice deep inside. And all has led to now."

"From the Black Wood," I muttered breathlessly.

"To the Red Thorn. From the center of the Black Circle to wings of the Silver Locust."

I tilt my head back onto Galen's billowing pillows.

"You'll be wanting to clean up," he suggested.

"In a moment," I replied. "Just a moment. Let me rest." I looked up to the ceiling in hopes that my eyes would be met with the sky once again, but all that was there was the wood and stone of the church's construction. I stared for a few minutes, praying it would open again so that I could feel the warmth and love and danger, but it didn't, so I closed my eyes, disappointed, and fell into a deep sleep.

Chapter 8

Sunday, November 6th 1695
The Flynn Residence
New Haven Harbor, Massachusetts
The Night of the New Moon

The events after my unbirthing were a blur to me. I had no recollection or remembrance of the measures Galen took to calm me, clean me, and get me home without detection of what had previously transpired. All I know is that it happened, and for all Douglas knew, I was unwell and needed to remain, undisturbed, in bed … for the child's sake, of course. Yes. The child's sake. The child who no longer swam in my belly.

Douglas was none the wiser, and as the doting husband and protective father-to-be that he was, he went to great lengths to ensure my comfort and well-being. Under his strict orders, I was not to be troubled or made upset. He allowed no one to visit with me—not Tansy, nor my mother, nor any of the other women I associated with in my sewing circle. Not even Galen, our priest holder. Yet, the only visitor he did permit in my chambers was the good Goody Olson who came a few days after my unfortunate tragedy bearing the gift of her herbal essence. I noticed a slight difference in the brew, and when I inquired about it, she hushed me and told me to lie still and get my rest.

I had felt weak and depleted, but after Goody's visit, I seemed to perk up tenfold. I got out of bed late in the afternoon and decided to surprise Douglas by preparing a lovely supper for us. I walked about the kitchen as the sun set quickly from the early autumn sky, and when there was total blackness, I rushed to the window and flung it wide open with hope in my heart—a hope to see my star-filled sky with the ripple leading to eternity churning in the center. Alas, it was not there, and my hope-filled heart sank like a stone. But my eyes did catch another sight—a curious one indeed. The Harmon Residence was directly next to us, and from my kitchen window, I could look directly into Goody Harmon's parlor. Douglas and I would often get a chuckle at seeing Mr. Harmon in his underclothes with his big belly wobbling about! There was always a candle burning somewhere in their home. With their maid and seven children always coming and going, there was constant noise, light and *something*. But tonight, there was silence. Darkness. Emptiness. Like a tomb. On moonless nights, I could always count on the illumination of the Harmon home to help light the darkness of the dirt road, but tonight was no such night.

Chapter 8

I squinted my eyes to try to get a better view of the outside world, when something else made me freeze in place. Two small figures manifested from the far end of the dirt path. Their dark shapes looked like black ink blots bouncing in the night. The shapes glided. Hovered. They moved slowly closer to the road. Faintly from the distance, a giggling din blanketed the air bringing back a memory of something Tansy said: *Winnie Gordon told me that two young children went missing over in Salem just last week.* But I could tell that what I was witnessing wasn't actual children per se, but more like ghostly figures silhouetted against the darkness.

A woman's cry rang out a few houses over— horrific screams that penetrated the silence. I went cold at the sound of the shrieks, for they had a deathly timbre to them like someone being murdered. One by one, lantern lights lit up across the landscape. Dogs howled. Bats fluttered from the disturbance in the night. Above the screams, the laughter from the figures filled my head, then the silhouettes vanished into thin air. I ran to the parlor, grabbed the lantern, and barreled out the front door to see what was going on. Others apparently had the same idea, as townsfolk from each road followed suit.

A few blocks over, Margaret Fletcher stood at her front gate. Her chubby fingers wound fiercely around a gold chain at her chest. It was obvious the screaming had come from her—beady eyes, puffy at the edges as if she had been crying for days, and her hair a mass of tangled, graying curls. She was frantic, yet speechless, as her husband cradled her shoulder.

As more and more lights glowed in front of the Fletcher home, it was clear to see what had terrified Goody Fletcher so—on her front lawn lay a severed goat's head wrapped in a vine of thorns. The legs of the animal were detached as well—two legs positioned in front of the head at an angle, two legs positioned at the back. No torso to be found in the vicinity.

The townspeople gasped and cried when they approached the scene. Goody Sheare fainted into her son's arms. Tansy ran to me with John at her side. "Is anyone hurt?" she asked.

"I don't think so," I replied.

She looked around at the faces of the crowd. "Where's Douglas?"

"Still at the jail. I suspect he'll be heading for home soon."

"Does anyone know what happened?" John roared above the crowd.

I shrugged my shoulders, and the people began shouting questions at Goody Fletcher, trying to piece together the events of the grisly scene. The clamor rose and came to a crescendo, and Mr. Fletcher raised his hand to try to bring peace, but it was no use, they were already infected with curiosity and fear, and the hysteria began to build.

After some time, two horses rode up to the Fletcher home—Jedidiah Gordon accompanied by Galen. The sight of him filled me with a tranquil light, and I realized how much I had missed him those last few days. He looked my way and gave a knowing smirk as he hopped down from his saddle and swiftly moved among the throng. When *he* raised his hand, the people quieted themselves, and my heart skipped a beat at his subtle display of power.

"Tell me true, Goody Fletcher," he said in a soothing voice, "what happened here?" His voice was like warm water washing over her, and her eyes glazed over with a faraway look to them.

"I can't quite say," she said calmly. "I was setting the table in the dining room when I heard a rustling outside. I walked to the window to see what was going on, and while nothing was in sight, I felt as if someone or *something* was... was... *watching* me." Her eyes grew wide at the memory. "And then I heard children giggling softly, and I figured it was those Prescott girls messing in my flower beds again. I marched to the front door, about ready to scold them, but... but when I threw open the door... I ... I..." She gasped and gripped her chain tighter.

Heads swung to Goody Prescott and her twin daughters Ellie and Emmie. She pulled them closer to her and proclaimed, "They were with me in prayer!"

A grumble arose, and attentions turned back to Reverend.

"The devil is here!" a voice sang. "The devil has come to New Haven!"

The grumble grew louder, and Tansy reached for my hand.

"Peace! Peace!" Galen exclaimed. "Let us not succumb to the hysteria that enveloped our dear neighbors. Let us be rational and without fear."

"Without fear?" Mr. Fletcher cried. "Reverend, this witchery came to my doorstep! Nearly gave my wife a heart attack!"

"Yes, Samuel, this is unfortunate, understandably. The fright that touched sweet Margaret is beyond compare, I would imagine. Remember, I too am not beyond the reach of mischief. My home was terrorized not so long ago. So collectively," he turned to face the throng, "we must assess the situation and handle it in the appropriate manner. We don't want to jump to conclusions, or make accusations, or..."

"There's a goat head on the Fletcher lawn. It was put there deliberately. What more is there to assess?" John Foster's deep voice growled and dripped with venom. I tugged at Tansy's arm and gave her a pleading look as if to say *make him stop; don't let him contribute to everyone getting worked up.*

She shrugged her shoulders and whispered, "He's got a point, Barbara," and with that, a steady stream of voices shouted over each other. I could scarcely make out what they said.

"Where are the Harmons?" a woman called out.

"Matthew Harmon has goats in a pen out back," someone muttered.

"I hear the younger Harmon girl suffers from an affliction. Bright red patches all over her arms,

like someone grabbed her with burning hot hands," someone else chimed.

"Devil's hands!"

"I saw a book at Goody Olson's that had words in Latin written on the spine," a woman declared sucking in her teeth.

The other woman standing next to her gave a hitch in her throat and brought her hand to her mouth. *"She has a goat too!"*

"We need to find whoever is doing this and put an end to their wickedness and trickery!"

"Trickery? This is clearly the sign of witchcraft."

"Thou shalt not suffer a witch to live."

I felt the madness descending quickly around me, and I squeezed Tansy's hand tighter as the ruckus from the crowd reached an overwhelming fever pitch. Desperately, I looked to Galen for some guidance. I pleaded with him with my eyes. In my head, I thought, *Stop them. Give them temporary pause.* And I think he heard me because he grimaced with agitation for a second then raised his hand again.

"Everyone! Everyone!" his voice rose above the crowd. "Let us stop this at once. At first light tomorrow, I will ride to Salem." Mouths dropped all around me. "There I will consult with the magistrate and their reverend and seek their counsel on how to deal with such instances. I want to get to the bottom of this just as much as you do. I trust you will remain calm and levelheaded in my absence, and not make any rash decisions while I seek the truth. While I am away, I will leave the chapel in the care of John and Temperance Foster. Services are suspended until I return, but for any other matters, please seek them out."

Tansy looked to me and nodded.

Galen went on to speak about volunteers for cleaning up the Fletcher's property, and he provided continuous reminders for civility in a time of fear, but I was suddenly distracted when Douglas raced up behind me and lifted me off the ground in a worried and protective embrace.

"Barbara! What's all this? Word got to me at the prison that something was going on. I came as quickly as I could."

John immediately informed Douglas of the situation as I relaxed my body against his. I had my eyes trained on Galen who closed out his oration with, "… keep your good thoughts flowing, and your actions to match." With that, the crowd dispersed back to their homes once again.

Galen scurried himself over to me and shook Douglas's hand heartily. "Mr. Flynn," he said with a stern look.

"Reverend," Douglas responded with a nod.

"I know you will take good care of the church, Tansy," Galen said. "You are the only one I feel comfortable to do so while I'm away."

"Of course, Father," she said. "I will do whatever you ask of me."

My face twisted as his words stabbed me deep. Did he not trust me?

Galen shook his head as if reading my mind again. "Douglas," he began, "I wish for Barbara to accompany me to Salem."

My heart stopped for a moment as Douglas's grip around me tightened.

"What for?" Douglas asked with a concerned tone.

Galen moved closer into our little circle and lowered his voice. There were still many people around us, and he looked over his shoulder often, ensuring no one else could hear. "I have to be honest with you," and we all moved in around him, "I fear for Barbara's safety. More specifically, I fear for the child's safety."

"Wait!" Tansy squealed. "Are we under attack? Is Barbara a target?"

"What are you talking about? What are you not telling us?" Douglas demanded.

Galen waved his hand in the circle and my eyes went blurry for a second. I know the others did as well, but it affected them more than me. I had seen and was aware of the power Galen possessed and had trained myself to see through the mirages. "You saw the people. Heard them. I don't wish any malicious or demonic harm should come her way, but that's certainly not what I mean. But them," he paused and craned his neck around, motioning to the collective mob, "there's no telling what's in the hearts and minds of men. Especially scared men spooked by the devil."

John lowered his eyes in shame.

"If she comes with me," he continued, "I can make sure she's kept safe. We'll leave at once, tonight. I'll drop her off in Mill Cove where I have kin who will take good care of her. I'll continue on to Salem, conduct my business there, then pick Barbara up on the way back."

I could sense Douglas's displeasure at the proposal. I, on the other hand, was infinitely intrigued. "There are other pregnant women in town, Father. Are you not concerned for them as well?" Douglas accused.

Galen smiled. "Absolutely. But I know the struggles Barbara has had to even be blessed in the womb. Goody Gordon would easily bounce back, and will, if tragedy were to strike. Barbara? Who knows? Do we want to take that chance? And besides, she is so very special to me. I value her opinion and her company, and she has served me and the church well. I've grown fond of her, and her absence this last week has been deeply felt by the congregation and me."

Douglas loosened his grip and spun me to face him. The thought of anything happening to his miracle child frightened him; it was written all over his face. "Do you think it best?" he asked.

I nodded. "Reverend makes a good point. I'm afraid, Douglas. After my illness, I don't want any more stress to come to the baby." I pushed my lower lip forward and placed my hands on my abdomen.

"Leaving tonight will cloak us in darkness. No one would know," Galen said.

"I'm still sick," I added. "I'm taking no visitors. The excitement of tonight's events set me back some."

Galen's eyes twinkled in approval of my deceptive suggestion. The gray waves in them crashed over a stony shore as I envisioned us wrapped together in a passionate embrace under the stars. A secret warmth filled my womanhood, and I desperately ached for him. Tansy bounced from foot to foot with grave concern, but I ignored her obnoxious and obvious gestures. She didn't need words to tell me she disapproved, and I truly didn't care.

Douglas looked to me, then to Galen, and back to me again. He put his hands on top of mine and sighed. And as his breath washed over me, I felt his body relax and give over to the power of Galen's words. *My* words.

Galen's spell.

My spell.

"Let's go home and get you ready, I suppose," Douglas said weakly.

"I'll do the same," Galen replied. "Then I'll come around your way, and we'll be off."

Chapter 9

Monday, November 7th 1695
The Open Road
Massachusetts
The Night of the New Moon

I collected some essential items, *Blodheksa* book included, and bid farewell to sweet Douglas. The apprehension on his face was undeniable, but another quick wave of Galen's hand seemed to quell his concerns, at least for the moment. The only living people who knew my whereabouts were Douglas, my sister, and her husband. I had a strange feeling that Tansy's loose lips would soon inform Winnie Gordon, but Galen assured me her silence would last at least the duration of our trip. The moment I climbed into the carriage, the horses spurred, and we began the journey south at a rapid pace. But after about an hour's time, he tugged at the reigns and turned the coach to the east.

East.

And we needed to remain south in order to get to Salem.

When my dearest friend Sarah Hutchings and I had sneaked away to Salem for the day, we had traveled south the entire way. I would never forget that day. Sarah was my oldest, most loyal friend. Yes, I had Tansy, my sister, as my constant confidante, but there was something special about the relationship between friends—friends who weren't kin. I understood the relationship I had with Sarah was much like the one Tansy shared with Winnie Gordon, and that was perfectly fine with me. Sarah had long, blonde, corn-silk hair that shimmered gold in the sunlight. It was so shiny that I swore I could see my reflection in it at the proper angle. A true beauty, she was—inside and out. I could tell Sarah anything my heart desired and not feel ashamed or less of a person for whatever thoughts were storming in my brain. So, when I had mentioned my curiosity about the hangings in Salem, Sarah never thought me odd for having such considerations. Be that as it may, Sarah felt the same way. Her brother Nathaniel had been born blind, and Sarah had been convinced her entire life that Goody Olson made a potion to make him see. She had revealed to me that her cousins in Lynn, a neighboring town to Salem, had been sending word to her about the allegations and trials since they had first begun!

It was understandable why she took an interest in these dark matters. She had a real concrete experience that would surely drive any person to investigate or be interested in the forces of the beyond. But me? I had no true justification for my curiosities. None. And that was peculiar and strange and blasphemous. I couldn't explain why I had taken such an interest in the unknown—I was just drawn to it, felt something different in my soul. I loved the darkness of the depths of the sea and the darkness in the heart of the forest. And my dreams always sang to me songs of ancient mystery. If anyone else known of my secret inclinations, I too would have surely been sent to Salem to be tried and hanged.

Sarah was the one to recommend we go and watch. I could scarcely contain my excitement at the suggestion. She was overly flirtatious with one of the stable boys, and a quick flash of what was under her dress with the promise of seeing more on our return was enough to convince him to hitch up a coach, tell the stable master he got word in Lynn about a mare for sale, and whisk us away to the gallows in time for the hangings.

And we headed south for the duration.

There was no shift to the east.

"We're not going to Salem, are we?" I said to Galen over the rush of the cold wind.

He lowered his jaw and eyed me from the side but remained focused on guiding the horses.

"You're not taking me to Mill Cove, are you?"

He shifted his eyes forward with nary a word to be said.

I smiled with sheer excitement. I don't know why, but the wind rushing through my hair, the cold blasting against my cheeks, the howling of wolves from the forest to the west of us, and the prospect of the sea to the east left me feeling giddy. Any other situation, any other moment, any other time, any other girl would have had cause to be concerned, cause to be alarmed, cause to be frightened even. But not I. I wasn't interested in staying with strangers in Mill Cove and waiting for Galen to return from his jaunt in Salem. I knew the lie. I was no longer with child. Based on that knowledge, there was simply no reason or explanation for my accompaniment on this trip. The turn east breathed new life into this clandestine outing.

"Rest," he commanded. "We'll be there soon enough."

He lifted his arm, and I placed my head in his lap. He brought his elbow down and leaned it against my back as he steered, locking me in place. The night sky was masked in wispy clouds, and the moon was invisible to the naked eye, yet I could feel it pulsating. I closed my eyes and did as he told me. The rocking of the coach, the throbbing of the obscure moon in the atmosphere, and fabric of Galen's trousers on my cheek lulled me to a short sleep.

My dreamless rest ended when we arrived some hours later at a small cottage on the edge of a bluff. Candles burned in the front room of the one-story structure, giving it an eerie glow from within. Trees surrounded it on all sides, yet I could hear the sea lapping at the stony shore in the not-too-far-away distance. I sat up and absorbed my surroundings. "You *did* bring me to Mill Cove," I declared.

"This isn't Mill Cove," he said, hopping down from the carriage.

I followed him and stayed close as we made our way to the door. "Then where?"

Again, he ignored my query. We took off our coats in the foyer and hung them on the rack by the door. Then he took my hand and led me through the candle glow of the hallway and into the kitchen at back of the home. A tall woman with long silver hair stood by the hearth. Her shapely figure wrapped in a black, gossamer dress cast shadows against the slow burning fire. When she turned to greet us, I struggled to decipher her countenance, for she looked fuzzy to my straining eyes. I decided it was the cold air and the long ride that made me weary, but still, I was able to interpret everything about her, save her face.

She beamed and outstretched her arms, accepting Galen's embrace. As she hugged him, I could tell she was watching me, looking at me from over his shoulder, her silver hair hanging long down her back, yet I still could not manage to see her face. What color were her eyes? Was she smiling at me? Grimacing? Was she soft and gentle, or hard and firm? I couldn't even determine if she was pretty or not! The suspense was maddening.

Their hold lasted a little longer than it should have, and I began to feel a twinge of jealousy arise in my chest, but they soon disengaged, and Galen stood in between us. "This is Blodwyn Solvven, she's kin to me," he introduced. "This is Barbara, the one I've written you about."

"Pleasure to make your acquaintance," I said.

Blodwyn nodded her head but said not a word. She outstretched her arm again and grabbed Galen's hand. Against the fire light, I saw black markings up and down her forearms. Ancient symbols that looked quite like the markings in the *Blodheksa* book were permanently emblazoned on her soft, milky flesh. A flash of familiarity washed over me, like I had seen this woman before, known her, seen her red blood spill from her wrists. But she walked Galen to a back room of the home, and I followed close behind, the thoughts melting from me with each step I took. Galen shut the door, and Blodwyn disappeared.

The room was lit throughout with black and white candles, and a bed was made up with gold and red blankets. I wanted to ask where he would be staying, but the words never did quite leave my mouth. I quickly came to understand that this was a room *we* would be sharing, and a warm rush invaded the space between my legs.

"She's beautiful, isn't she?" he said as he moved to the bed.

"I... I couldn't really tell," I confessed. "My vision is blurry from the night and the long ride and the..."

He chuckled ominously, and it stabbed me with childish shame. "You just can't see yet. I understand."

Confused, I turned my back to him and moved to the window at the opposite side of the room.

"There aren't any stars tonight," he said. "And the moon…"

"Yes. The new moon," I said under my breath, gazing out the cold pane of glass.

"They won't move for you yet. You need to see first."

I spun around and faced him. "What does that mean? I don't understand."

He patted a space on the bed next to him beckoning me to sit. I crossed my arms at my chest and clutched the tops of them to try to warm myself before taking my seat across from him. He pulled the *Blodheksa* book from his pastor's cloak and set it gently in between us.

My eyes went wide. "How did you?" I began, but I soon realized he must have procured it from my satchel while I was asleep.

He placed one hand on the top of the book and one hand on top of mine, and in an instant, I was no longer cold, for a fire swelled up throughout my arm and into the very core of my body. "Have you ever asked yourself what it is you truly want?" he said.

"What do you mean?"

"From life. What is your purpose?"

"Well," I said, "by that measure, what is the purpose of any man? You're a man of God, yet here we are. I know this isn't godly or godlike. This place, this book, what I've seen you do..."

"Oh, but it is, Barbara," he interrupted. "It is godly, the things I can do. The things *you* can do."

"Just not the reverend's God."

He raised his eyebrows with a cunning sneer. "More or less. But God all the same."

I pulled back a little, but he strengthened his grip on my hand, keeping me in place.

"You never answered the question, Barbara. What do you truly want from life? Have you ever even contemplated it?"

I paused and thought about the inquiry. And I knew. I knew that my wants and desires were not of this world. Sure, I wanted the loving husband, the happy home, the darling children, but those were wants that had been instilled upon me from birth. To peel back the conscious level of actual needs, it was much more complicated and involved than the simple trivial ponderings of a provincial girl. For there was a need, a deep-seated longing. The inevitable and eventual. "I know what I want right now," I said and looked to the book.

"Ah!" he sighed. "You can feel its power, but to know its words is something entirely different."

"Can you teach me?" I asked.

He shook his head. "I'm afraid not. Only you can unlock those mysteries for yourself."

His words were like honey—sweet with a stinging aftertaste and singing with the buzz of the summer bees. He picked up the book from the bed and placed it on the nightstand beside it. Then he reached over and brushed the side of my face with the side of his hand. "You are the new moon, Barbara. The new moon to wax to completion and open the doors of paradise."

I stirred on the inside, placed my hands high up on both of his thighs, and shifted closer to him. He lowered his head and nuzzled in the crook between the base of my neck and my shoulder, smelling me, breathing me in, inhaling my essence. His hot breath was like fire to my skin— fire that burned away all my sins and indiscretions. He made me new. His lips gently grazed along the side of my neck with gentle kisses until he reached my earlobe and used his teeth to pull it into his mouth to suckle. The loud sucking noises in my head made hen-flesh dance on my skin, and I felt myself falling, melting, succumbing to his touch. He moved his hand up the length of my dress and stopped at my breasts, cupping them, kneading them, as I moved my hands farther up his legs to the center of his core and drew along the outline of his manhood beneath his trousers.

Suddenly, the door creaked open, and hurriedly I pulled away from the sin. Galen gave a small laugh. "No need to be shy, Barbara. It's just Blodwyn."

I struggled to say something in protest, but the door opened wider, revealing Blodwyn in the threshold. Her long silver hair draped down over her shoulders, covering the upper part of her naked body. The voluptuous curves of her womanly figure bounced from beneath the locks. Her arms dipped low below her waist, and her hands covered the glistening curls of her white sex. I stirred again, surprising even myself at my physical reaction to this creature.

"She is beautiful, isn't she," Galen said, and it was more of a statement than a question. There was no way to deny it; Blodwyn was a vision, although I still had difficulty with translating the actual features of her face. I nodded in wonder as she glided across the room and approached us on the bed. Galen took leave of his position on the bed and made his way to the floor. Blodwyn stood next to me and pushed my shoulders back, forcing me to lie on my back. I was frozen in place. Unable to move. Unable to speak. Utterly in awe at the scenario unfolding before me.

She lifted a leg up and straddled me on the bed, then took my arms and placed them above my head. With a sweeping motion of her shoulders, her hair swept behind her, revealing the full view of her body. Her skin was alabaster white, as if it had never been kissed by the sun, as if it had been quenched in the brightest moonlight since the beginning of time. Her dense breasts heaved with her every breath, causing me to stare even harder at them. And just as I had suspected, symbols, like those in the *Blodheksa* book, adorned both of her arms.

Blodwyn bent her upper torso forward and came down upon me, face to face. Her warm breath buzzed on my lips, and when she clamped her mouth unto mine, it was gentle, like kissing the pale petals of the jasmine flower. Her mouth was warm and wet with a vague flavor of dark rum. When her tongue danced along the surface of mine, it was intoxicating. My head changed and shifted and danced with the movements of the open and close, open, and close. I was lost, but not so lost that I wasn't committed to the here and now.

Amidst the kisses that burned with flowery passion, Blodwyn extended her hand behind her, gathered the fabric of my pinafore to my waist, and exposed my nakedness. Galen stood up and walked to the other side of the bed, closer to Blodwyn and me, so he could see good and well in the candlelit room. Suddenly, I felt Blodwyn's hand rub along the inside of my bare thigh while Galen's hand worked its way up my other. My secret area, which wasn't so secret at that moment, was swollen and dripping in the creases of my flesh. First, one of Blodwyn's smooth and silky fingers slipped inside of me, followed shortly thereafter by one of Galen's rough and thick ones. My entire body tensed up from the surprise of their pillaging as my mind tried to reconcile right from wrong, moral from immoral, pleasure from sin. Ultimately, I gave in when my body shivered, as blasts of pleasure waves rocked me. Behind my closed eyes, I could see the stars and the moon and the tear in the sky with its swirling colors of pinks and purples and greys. They both plunged simultaneously, together driving me higher and higher to an ecstasy I'd only known in my dreams. Mindlessly, I brought one hand down from above my head and reached for Blodwyn's breast. I took it in my hand, felt its robust weight, took her pale pink nipple between my fingers, and squeezed. She was cold, like a layer of frost encompassed her body, and my hands were like fire against her ice. Blodwyn squealed a familiar sound of pleasure, as I bit her lower lip and tugged more firmly at her breast. Galen slipped his free hand underneath the space between Blodwyn and my raised dress and returned the motion on my chest that I had imparted on Blodwyn. As he wildly groped me on top, his finger on the inside of me became two. He scissored them around Blodwyn's, so the three digits moved in and out and inside of me as one. They both tickled the soft pad of my inside sex until I could no longer stand it. I threw my head back, breaking Blodwyn's kiss and releasing her breasts from my grip, and I let the pulsing waves push me farther and farther out to sea. I rose, on the inside, and held my breath until it felt like a wave crashed down on their fingers.

They both exited me, and Galen smoothed down my dress as Blodwyn hopped from the bed. Her hair was a tangled mess in front of her face, and when she straightened herself out, I was able to catch a glimpse of her visage. I was finally able to see and determine the features of her face. Her familiarity became all too clear.

And my heart stopped. My breath hitched in my throat. Again, I stammered and stuttered with the words. Galen smiled, and I watched as Blodwyn glided to the door in her naked splendor. I watched as she reached for the doorknob. I watched as her body dissipated into a funnel of white smoke before she was ever able to cross the threshold.

"Me?" I managed to croak.

Galen nodded.

"*Me*?" I screamed as I sat up in the bed.

He nodded again. "How else are you to know thyself?"

My hand flew to my mouth. "I... I... I don't understand! How could that have been..."

"From another time, another moment. Plucked from the fabric of existence. To *know* and know you in a way that only you can."

"I still don't understand. I can't."

Galen picked up the *Blodheksa* book and handed it to me. "Yes, you do. You understand full well now."

I held the book and fanned out the pages. No longer were there runes and ancient text. There were words. Actual words! I flipped back to the front page and read out loud, "The powers of the Blood Witch..." I stopped and put the book down.

Galen reached his hand out and grabbed for me. "You understand now, Barbara?"

"More than ever."

Chapter 10

Tuesday, November 8th 1695
Galen's Cottage by the Sea
Massachusetts
The Afternoon of the Waxing Crescent Moon

Although a drop of spirits had never passed my lips, I felt drunk when I arose the next morning. After what had transpired between Galen and Blodwyn and me, I was still trying to piece together the reality and the fantasy. At one point during the night, I had gotten much too warm. I removed my pinafore and lay underneath the heavy quilt naked. I had fully convinced myself that I was ill, sick with fever, and Galen was transporting me to a physician in a neighboring town where I was going to die, and everything that happened was merely a fever dream, a hallucination! That explanation would have been much too easy, though. As I've learned in life, the truth was never easy, even when it felt like a lie.

Regardless, now that the words were made known to me, I had spent the rest of the evening sitting up in the bed hungrily reading the

Blodheksa book. Page after page, I devoured every word presented before me like a starving man at a feast. Everything made sense and didn't at once. Even though I was now privy to the actual deciphering of what was being said, there was still so much I didn't understand. Galen lay next to me throughout the night watching me flip and read, flip and read. Occasionally, I would pause to ask him a question, to which he would smile, shake his head, or tell me to "keep going. I can't help you." It was frustrating, but I soon understood this was something I needed to solve on my own.

My own, indeed. The book spoke to me, sang to me. As I read each sentence, it was as if someone were reading it to me from afar—from a long-ago forgotten land in a voice that was deep and guttural, harsh to my ears yet soothing at the same time. And when the sentences came together on the page, I heard music in the distance—the beating of a deerskin drum throbbing rhythmically against the sounds of a bell-like chime and a woman singing a sort of lullaby. There were instructions for spells and glamours, and outlines for rituals for all sorts of things—worshipping the moon, celebrating the harvest, asking the higher power for favor and material things. All very familiar. Not so quite off from the asks and wants and desires of my own community. We, too, celebrated harvest and made requests of the Lord. "Is this all real?" I turned to ask Galen.

"Do you feel that it is?"

"Deeply, yes. It just doesn't seem like it could be."

"Anything can be," he answered, and I noticed his eyes were drifting to sleep.

"What's a glamour?" I asked.

"It's a mask. A parlor trick. But it's temporary. When you want someone to think something or see something that truly isn't there, you use a glamour."

"Like what you did with Winnie in the church?"

"Yes, Barbara."

"Like how you convinced Douglas to let me ride with you?"

"Mmm hmm," he droned sleepily.

"Was Blodwyn a glamour?"

"No, Barbara. Blodwyn is something else."

He rolled over on his side, indicating that he would no longer answer any of my questions. Within seconds, his breaths became deep and heavy as they snarled their way out from his nose.

Midway through the book there was a story, and that was oddly familiar too: The tale of the Blood Witch who brought the Blood Brother and Blood Sister into the world, and they drenched the land with the blood of the people. From that newly consecrated land, a garden arose from the depths of the underworld, and paradise was reformed on Earth. The New Eden. I quickly closed the book when it got to the part of the twisted trees with human limbs sprouting from the trunk, for I felt like I could only take so much, and the story was starting to go down a very dark path. I had so many questions to ask of Galen but dared not disturb him in his slumber. I knew what his answers would be, anyway—they would not be answers I wanted or needed, so it was best I tried to figure it out on my own rather than suffer the frustration of ambiguity.

I placed the book on my chest and stared at the ceiling, hoping that staring at the wooden beams would help to relax my mind and drift me to sleep. But in my conscious mind, all I could picture was Blodwyn on top of me, kissing me, writhing against me with her womanly curves, sliding her finger into my most secret place. In the eyes of God and the community, I was now an adulterer—an offense punishable however the courts saw fit. If anyone found out, I could be whipped in the streets and forced to wear a letter on my clothing to indicate my crimes like Mary Mendame, or I could be put to death like Mary Latham. The tales of the two Marys were as old as I could remember, but they served their purpose for all women, and their children, and their children's children, to serve and obey their husband as the one and only. But how would they know? No one was going to know. For all anyone knew, I was still pregnant with my husband's child and there was no proof or evidence of any fornication with the reverend or his kin.

Me.

Me?

That piece of information I tucked away deep into my mind, for it was hard for me to resolve

that as fact. It was more fiction to me than anything. How could the one called Blodwyn Solvven
be *me*? It didn't make sense. It wasn't possible.
And if it was me, why would I do those... those
indecent things to *myself*? I'd never been attracted
to women, nor was I still. Yes, I was one who was
able to appreciate the beauty held by the female
gender. I was always able to compliment and offer
my delight in the female form. It was more of an
admiration for the many gifts given to my sisters
from the Lord Himself. Like Sarah Hutchings—I
always recognized her beauty with wonder and
awe, but never had I felt the sexual attraction or
desire to touch her or be with her in the most profane of ways. And Winnie Gordon—while I could
not stand her as a human being, I would never
deny that she had been blessed with beauty from
the Lord as well. But never had I wanted to kiss
her mouth or take her breasts in my hands.

Never, until Blodwyn. Blodwyn delighted me
in the most arcane way. There was a sort of savagery that erupted from deep within when she
kissed me and touched me. I felt as if I wanted
to consume her entirely, make her incorporate
with me somehow, be one with her dominance
and essence. She unlocked mysteries in me that I
didn't even know existed. And as I lay in the bed,
staring at the ceiling, I longed for her to come
back to me. I ached for her to touch me and kiss
me and open me up some more.

But, if Blodwyn was me, and I was doing those
things to myself, was it truly adultery? Had Galen

not been in the equation, would I still be considered an adulterer? I was not naïve; I had brothers, and I knew what boys did to pleasure themselves when they became of age and were alone. Was this not the same thing? I finally fell asleep, but it was not restful, nor peaceful, as there were too many things filling my head at once.

…hence why I woke up feeling slightly drunk.

I threw my arm across the bed and felt the empty space beside me. Galen was gone, and on top of his pillow lay my book. For a second, I felt lost and confused, abandoned almost, but the book called to me and quelled my anxieties. If Galen had left me alone in this cabin to die, I knew I was going to be fine.

But he hadn't. The moment I reached for the book to continue reading, he came through the door carrying a satchel around his shoulder.

"Good morning," I greeted him.

"It's mid-day, Barbara." He smiled.

"Mid-day! Impossible!"

"Possible. We had a long ride and a long night. I let you sleep until your heart's content. I figured you would need the rest. I've been awake for some hours now."

"Are we riding for Salem today?" I asked.

His face screwed up in confusion. "Salem? I thought you were well informed of our true intentions."

My cheeks flushed hot, and I brought the quilt to my chin to hide my silliness. "I… I wasn't sure if…"

"It's quite alright," he said, and he smiled at me again, putting my shame to ease. He laid the satchel on the spot beside me, let his coat drop to the floor, sat at the foot of the bed, and caressed my ankles from underneath the quilt.

I shivered from his touch. "Freezing!" I exclaimed. "Where did you go? You're so very cold!"

He chuckled softly through his closed-smile mouth. "I needed to get a few things. And yes, it is very cold out there, which is why I plan on us staying inside the rest of the evening."

"But won't they be expecting us back tomorrow? Shouldn't we be leaving during the night?"

"A storm will cause our delay."

"Storm?"

As the word left my lips, the steady pelting of rain thrashed against the roof of the cottage and whipped the single-paned window. Galen looked at me and smiled. "Storm," he confirmed.

I smiled back and eased myself deeper into the comfort of the bed. "Could it storm every day?" I asked dreamily.

"I'm afraid not," he replied solemnly.

I reached my arms above my head and gave a little squealing sound as my limbs stretched and creaked. "Will Blodwyn be returning?"

"I'm afraid not," he repeated and shimmied his body farther onto the bed.

I scooted over to provide him with some more space, and a new tension rose between us. He certainly was handsome to look at—more handsome than any man I'd ever seen with a finely drawn jaw and a hard body beneath his priestly robes. I had often wondered what he looked like in the flesh—envisioned it in my dreams, thought about it in my daytime musings. Every time he had drawn me in for an embrace, my mind would trace the outline of his figure, then erase all notion of garments above *and* below the waist! Adulterous thoughts, yes. Adulterous dreams, absolutely. And so, in that room, adulterous acts were set to take place as the culmination of my wants and desires.

My spell.

He moved his hands up my calves and set them on my knee tops, and I eyed him, questioning him with my expression. *What are you doing?* My eyes said to him.

"Whatever it is you want," he replied and spread my legs gently apart.

I nodded automatically, for every dream I had ever had of being with him was happening all at once, and I was too weak to stop it from coming to fruition. Too weak and too willing.

"Are you hungry?" he asked, and I thought it odd for him to question my need or want for sustenance at that very moment.

I thought about it for a second. "No," I replied.

He threw the quilt from the bed, exposing the full view of my nakedness. He widened my legs farther apart and wiggled himself at the edge of me. His hands slid from my knee-tops and up to

Chapter 10

my inner thighs to where his fingertips tickled the outer region of my harbor of hope. It was sticky with my desire. "No?" he questioned. "Feels like you're hungry."

I sighed heavily, and before I could respond, Galen closed in on me and buried his face between my legs. The warmth of his tongue against my treasure cancelled out the cold from within the room. My hips moved with every kiss of his mouth, every jab of his tongue, every nip of his teeth against my center pearl. My feet became tingly and numb from the pleasure, and I moaned in spite of myself, for this type of fornication I had no knowledge—only gossip and speculation. Sarah Hutchings had told me once how she let the stable boy kiss her there, and when he had brought her to climax in his mouth, she was left feeling embarrassed and ashamed. Yet, I felt no embarrassment as Galen lapped at me heartily, taking me closer and closer to the edge of ecstasy. I felt no shame as I reveled in gratification from this new form of pleasure. I was swept away in the sensations of his hands grabbing my hips, his hair tickling my stomach, and his mouth kissing me so hard in the most sacred of places. "Seems like you're the hungry one," I whispered. It was meant to be an inside thought, but in the moment of passionate frenzy, the words escaped my lips.

Galen quickly stopped, to my displeasure, and knelt up on the bed. Without a word, he untied the laces of his trousers and dropped them far enough to reveal his veiny beast. I think my jaw fell slightly at the sight of him, and I planted the balls of my feet steadily into the mattress and arched my hips in invitation. No sooner had I spread myself for him, he was upon me, inside me, thrusting wildly within, stroking my fires with reckless abandon. The ecstatic edge he had brought me to with his mouth had once more been reached, and he threw me over it again and again, wave after climactic wave, my honey coating him to the hilt of his shaft. But there was an urgency in the act. With each thrust, with each jab, I felt as if he detached more and more from me. There was a faraway look in his eyes as if he had expected something more, longed for something more—as if this was more mission than desire. By the end, I don't know if he realized I was even there. He made sure to empty himself as I rose on my final wave, and when he was finished, he slithered out and to the other side of the bed. I threw my arm across his chest and rested my head on his shoulder.

After a few minutes, he asked, "Are you hungry?"

I paused, contemplating the question again. "No," I replied. "Should I be?"

"I would assume eventually," he answered and drew out a long and agitated sigh.

I woke up to the howling of the storm outside the cabin. The tempest Galen had spoken of earlier was in full swing with the wind thrashing against the outer walls and the relentless rain pounding down on the roof. The sounds echoed in the dark room, and I rose from the bed, wrapped the quilt about my shoulders, and walked to the window to observe the spectacular show. Through the blasts of near horizontal rain, the night sky dazzled with a thousand stars and the sliver of silver as the moon waxed slightly with its thin smile. I peered over my shoulder at Galen on the bed. He had removed his clothing before falling asleep earlier, and I watched as the dark outline of his chest rose and fell with each heavy breath of slumber. A disappointed feeling darkened my heart. My imaginings had never portrayed to me a disconnected Galen, and even though he had fulfilled my most secret of hidden and carnal dreams, I felt he was miles away from me. Had I not been good enough? Had I displeased him? Did he not feel pleasure from our union? Did he regret the act?

I walked back to the bed, and as I did, my foot kicked something in the darkness. I bent down to see what it was, and to no surprise, it was the *Blodheksa* book lying next to the satchel Galen had brought in with him earlier. I took the book into my hands and cradled it close to my bare chest. Immediately, I heard the voice, the song. It soothed me. Lulled me. Renewed my spirit with courage and purpose. I asked the book, and it replied—I was not a failure to my lover, and I was being silly and immature to think such things. I placed *Blodheksa* on the nightstand and opened Galen's pack. Therein were curious things: black candles, rocks and shells from the shore, and a knife—to the average eye, these things wouldn't make sense to be sharing the same space, but to me, on instinct, I knew just what to do.

I lit the room up with the candles. Strategically placed them in each corner to create a golden glow throughout. Galen's body on the bed came into view, and I stood over him, knife in one hand, and with my other, I ran my fingers up and down his barrel chest. His manhood sprang at attention at my touch, yet he still slept—dreamily breathing in some far-off fantasy world. However, I was determined to deal not in fantasies. With the knife, I sliced across his arm in the crook of his elbow—the natural line that separates forearm from upper arm bloomed with tiny blood bubbles. His eyes shot open from the fire of the sting, and immediately, I knelt beside him and took his arm in my mouth, sucking at the wound. I let the metallic flavor dance on my tongue before I swallowed it down.

My nether region throbbed furiously, and I nearly exploded sans touch, so I straddled his waist and guided his shaft into me, where I held him inside me, motionless, allowing him to pulse on my inside like a heartbeat in my loins. I handed him the knife, and with his free hand, he clawed at my breast, squeezing it, tugging it. He lifted it up, and with the knife drew a line across the flesh of the underside. I squealed from the pain, and he sat up to suckle at my breast, only it was my blood he lapped and licked.

With one swoop, he lifted me off him, and he placed me on the bed on all fours and grabbed one of the candles. He stood behind me, and in no time, the melted wax from the black candle scorched the flesh of my back. He moved his arm at five points, and then completed it with a circular motion. My skin sizzled, and my body wriggled from the heat, but I was bent over before him in supplication and was branded—the five-pointed star hardened and sealed on to me. He placed the candle back on the nightstand, put his hands on my hips, and plunged deep into me. The lion and the lioness. I bowed farther down to accept his full length and he drove me hard into the quilt, my face plastered into the mattress. I could feel his hand caressing the outline of the star on my back as he grunted and groaned in delight. I squealed too, as that sensation took over again. It climbed higher in me, rising in me. I used my sex to clamp down against him, and that excited him more, heightened his pleasure, and made him quicken his pace.

From the corner of my eye, I caught a glimpse of the outside world. The rain continued its heavy assault on the cottage, but the sky beyond had changed. Shifted. The waxing moon smiled at me, and I cried out, "The stars have moved!"

Galen stopped briefly to sneak a peek out the window, and I heard him gasp. And the frenzy of our affair ended. He slid back into me with a slow, gentle motion, and continued to ease in and out with tender, deliberate thrusts. With every plunge, the stars gathered closely together in the sky until they formed what appeared to be a giant circle. With every thoughtful and loving insertion, the circle grew wider, like a ripple tearing the sky in half. Like the night I lost the baby. My heart filled with such happiness, and I longed to rise into the circle in the sky, punch through the world, and see beyond the beyond—all with Galen mounting me like a proper beastly lover. "We could go together and split open the world," I whispered.

Slowly, he pulled back, almost completely released from my body, with just the tip of him tickling my opening. "We will," he said, and drove himself deep and hard before he released himself into my depths.

His upper body descended on top of me, and he kissed the waxy remnants of the five-pointed star on my back before exiting and lying back down on the bed. I walked over to the window again to gaze at the sky. The circle was gone, but the moon still smiled at me—the thin, knowing smile of the universe blessing me with her approval.

Some time had passed, and I assumed Galen had fallen back asleep. I couldn't. I couldn't sleep anymore. I was restless and worked up, like I could have crawled out of my own skin. I had been cooped up in this room for too long. I wanted to explore. Wanted to use the outhouse. Wanted a bath. Wanted...

"Are you hungry now?" Galen said, breaking into my thoughts.

Again, I paused, pondering the question. Slowly, a low rumble worked its way up from the pit of my stomach, and a slow ache filled me with a feeling of emptiness—an emptiness I had never felt before, for I had never known real hunger my entire life. And this? This was something surreal. Something quite different. Something unnatural. I looked at Galen on the bed and remembered how his blood tasted as I drank the remnants of his life force. I scraped my tongue along the roof of my mouth to try to savor any remaining droplets. The growl from my gut grew louder in the quiet room, and I winced with a hint of slight embarrassment. I could deny it no longer.

"Yes," I replied. "As a matter of fact, I'm quite ravenous."

Chapter 11

Thursday, November 10th 1695
The Meeting House
New Haven Harbor, Massachusetts
The Afternoon of the Waxing Crescent Moon

In the deep, dark forest, the trees swayed and danced. Their silhouettes against the black as ink sky with the smiling moon cast shadows that filtered between their gangly, majestic arms. I felt safe under the protection of those shadows. I wandered for some time, lingered among the dark spots, and caressed the trunk of each tree I passed. A low roar echoed in the night, its sound not of the human or animal kind, but mechanical, grinding. It made the leafless trees bend and shiver. Quickly, I came to understand this wasn't the Black Wood that I knew so well. I searched for my special clearing to no avail. This place was another wood, from another place, and quite possibly another time.

I came to a section of trees surrounded by a mass of piled up leaves. Next to it was a burned-out fire. The smoke smell hung heavy in the air indicating that the person or persons who made the fire had only recently put it out and left. I wondered if they were still in the vicinity, so I looked about anxiously, but I could sense no other human presence. A buzzing noise grew louder in my head, and I walked closer to the leaf pile. Flies swarmed frantically around it. I picked up a large stick and poked and prodded at the heap, and this upset the flies some! With each stab of my stick, the leaves fell away, until ultimately, I uncovered a dead body underneath the foliage. But it wasn't really a body. I'd seen death before— seen what a dead body looks like when the life has been extinguished from behind their eyes. This was just a mass. A hunk of stinking meat. It resembled more a large, slaughtered sow than a person. But I knew it was a person—had been a person. The wind blew up again and a voice spoke to me from the trees: *An unfinished dissection of flesh. A mass of unrecognizable decomposition.*

I moved closer to get a better look at the decay, to make out the shape of the body or anything else to indicate what had happened there. I needed to see it. I needed to smell it. I needed to hear the pattern of the flies as they hummed around the once person. A breeze blew by, and it carried the pungent smell of rot to my opened mouth. I winced when the aroma grabbed me in the back of the throat but was soon unaffected by the offensive smell. I tasted it. I tasted the decay on the roof of my mouth and the back of my throat. It tasted like suffering and a thousand screams.

He screamed a thousand times. The voice called out again, harsh and guttural, like the voice I heard in Galen's cabin, the voice that called to me from beyond the book. I closed my eyes, relaxed my body, and a surge of energy came jolting up from the pit of my stomach. The familiar feeling of levitating off the ground overwhelmed me. I fell to my knees at the feet of the body and touched it.

I looked upward to the sky in hopes to see the smiling moon. Maybe she would give me the answers of whom this person had been, who had done this to him, and why had this all happened, but I saw not the night sky or the clouds or the moon; I saw only the ripple in the center of the tree line — the mass of unified stars gathered in a cluster to break the seal of the worldwide open. It was there, but it was quiet and still. It didn't pulsate or glow or give any indication that the mouth of it was widening. It was frozen in time, frozen in place, like it had started to open, but something stopped it in its tracks, and it never got a chance to come to fruition.

It never got a chance to be born, the voice said, this time closer and more distinct.

I reached down and touched my abdomen, and I wept for the dead and for the unborn. So much loss, so much pain. Suddenly, a crow flew onto one of the low hanging branches of the tree next to where the body lay. I looked up at it, at its piercing red eyes glowing in the twilight of the forest. Its black feathers shimmered iridescently, like an oil slick hitting the sunlight and reflecting greens and yellows and browns and golds. His eyes spoke to me in that guttural voice—that same guttural voice that had been haunting me for weeks now... for months... for my whole life somehow. The crow cawed, and I was filled with peace. I stood up and reached my hand to him, beckoning him to perch on my arm, to walk by my side and take refuge in my company. He understood me and flitted down from his branch, but as soon as he came into my range, his wings stopped flapping. They went frozen and still mid-air, as if something had seized his little heart, and his body plummeted to the ground and to the hunk of death by the trees.

You are death, the voice sang, and a great tumult descended from the sky as a thousand crows barreled out from behind the trees and swarmed together to attack me. They intended to pluck my eyes from my face and my tongue from my mouth and add them to the collection of body parts in the pile, but I raised my hands to my face, outstretched them both in the space before me, and like the first unfortunate crow, the thousand of them froze in mid-air at once and tumbled to the earth at my feet.

You are death, the voice screamed, and I woke up with a fright.

My body jolted hard against Galen's lap in the carriage. We had been riding back home all through the night, and he bid me to rest in the early hours. The sun was close to rising, but it was still frigid cold, so I wasn't about to pass up the chance to keep warm. At the time of his suggestion, I hadn't been tired, but as soon as my head sank into his soft trousers and I closed my eyes, there was no stopping the sleep from invading my body.

Now, I sat up sharply at attention, still reeling from my dream.

"What vexes you?" he asked, keeping his eyes on the dirt road.

"Just a dream, just a dream," I answered, trying to push it out of my mind.

"Ah," he sighed, "and when wilt thou learn that for *us,* dreams aren't just dreams? They are sometimes mirrors reflecting to us our true nature and feelings. They are sometimes visions showing us events that have not yet come to pass. They are sometimes admonitions cautioning us about uncertain dangers. And they are sometimes gateways transporting us to other places and times, like catching glimpses of the universe from different vantage points."

"Could they be all four?"

He pondered for a moment. "I don't see why not."

"Are we far from home?"

"No. It won't be much longer now. I expect we'll make it back right after daybreak."

"Good. They've made a mess while we were gone. There's much to clean up."

Tansy and Douglas were waiting for us at my home when we arrived sometime later. For a second, I thought it odd that my sister had stayed with my husband, as a guest, in my absence. I didn't have time to dwell on it further when they began to explain what had been happening in the good town of New Haven Harbor.

"We thought you would be returning yesterday!" Tansy exclaimed.

"My apologies," I said. "There was a storm. It was much too dangerous to take the horses out and make the trek, so we stayed an extra night in Mill Cove with the reverend's cousin." The lie oozed from my lips so smoothly.

"I was going to send the stable boy down to Salem to bring word to you," Douglas added. "But everything here happened so quickly, I knew you would be back before he would make it there."

Galen eyed me casually. "Explain what happened," he said.

"Right after you left, right at sunrise, another grisly scene appeared," Tansy began. "This time on Goody Olson's property."

Douglas paced the parlor floor, slapping the pockets of his trousers. "Crows. Hundreds of them. All dead. Lined up on her porch, her steps, her lawn. A line of their carcasses leading straight to her front door."

I paused, remembering my dream.

"Cats. Goats. Crows," Douglas continued. "What's next? People?"

"Stop!" I admonished. "There has to be an explanation to all…"

"Witchcraft!" Tansy blurted. "Don't you see? This is the work of the dark one! The devil himself!"

Galen moved closer to her and put a hand on her shoulder in hopes of calming her down. "Easy, Tansy. Easy. You know the implications of those accusations. There's no need to let this spiral into something it need not be."

"It's too late for that, Reverend," Douglas said, his voice shaking with fear.

"What do you mean?" I interjected. "What do you mean, too late?"

"At mid-day. The magistrate will hear testimony. A complaint has been made against Goody Olson."

"What?" I exclaimed in disbelief. "Goody Olson is our midwife! This is preposterous! Who lodged the complaint?"

Tansy's back stiffened, and she hung her head low. "Winnie did," she whispered, and I huffed with anger.

Galen stood as quiet as a statue.

"It's just a preliminary, informal hearing," Tansy said. "With all the strange happenings, and now this complaint…"

"Reverend," Douglas said, "was your trip to Salem fruitful? Did you gain any new insight that could perhaps help the magistrate in today's proceedings?"

Galen nodded. "Yes, yes. I should head over there right away and inform him on what I've learned."

Douglas turned to me with a look of genuine concern on his face. "And you, Barbara? You and the baby are alright?"

"Quite well, thank you," I assured. "Reverend Galen's kin were most kind and attentive." I patted my abdomen. "The little seashell is perfectly fine."

He smiled with relief. "Thank you," he said to Galen.

Galen nodded tersely and left.

By the afternoon, it seemed as if the entire town had gathered in the meeting hall. Galen sat next to the magistrate at the main table, and the room went silent as he banged his gavel down.

"Order! Order!" he boomed, but the audience didn't need that directive as they had been church mice the second the gavel hit the desk. Magistrate looked nervous. His long, horse face was wrought with anguish and doubt. "Today we are gathered to hear the testimony of Goody Olson. This is an unprecedented proceeding, a cautionary inquiry. The intention of this meeting is only to determine if further action is necessary in the investigation of the most recent community events. This is not a trial. I repeat: This is not a trial. I have consulted with the good reverend here, and we have determined that he will assist me with the inquest. This is leaning toward that of a religious nature, and who best to carry out the will of the Lord? Reverend Galen has assured me that his recent journey to Salem, and his meeting with their council has given him some new and interesting insight on how to go about handling the recent occurrences in New Haven Harbor. We are determined, as a community, to take all the preventative measures possible to not go through what our brothers and sisters in Salem did. Without further delay, will the guard please bring out the witness to begin the review?"

The door behind the magistrate's desk swung open, and Douglas escorted Goody Olson to the witness stand. Goody Olson hobbled up the step and sat down in the seat. She folded her wrinkly hands in front of her and breathed in deeply. Fear was absent from her eyes as she smiled brightly at the people in the crowd.

"Please state your name for the record," Magistrate began. A low murmur arose from the audience, and although the magistrate said this wasn't a trial, it sure was starting to feel like one.

"Eliza Olson," she said happily.

"As you know, someone has made allegations against you of the most heinous kind. This inquiry is just a precaution to determine the nature of these claims and if any further investigation is needed. Do you understand why your testimony today is needed?"

"I do." She smiled, unfazed.

"Excellent, let us proceed. Is your husband still living?"

"No," she replied.

"And children?"

"I never bore a single one. But you know this, don't you, John Williams," she said with a sarcastic sneer.

The crowd gave a chuckle, and the magistrate shifted in his chair.

"What is your occupation here in New Haven Harbor?"

"I am the midwife and the physician for the women."

"And what are the specifics of your work?"

"Well, I do much in the ways of women's care. First and foremost, I take care of the expectant mothers and deliver the children. But my work is so much more than that. I instruct the new mothers on the ways of caring for the babes. I guide the young girls when they bloom into womanhood. I also take care of the aging women and assist them with any problems they may have of a womanly kind. But you knew that too, Magistrate. As I recall, I was just recently at your home on a call of concern for your wife, Goody Williams, and…"

Nervously, he banged the gavel on the desk as the crowd's laughter swelled in the hall.

"Thank you, Goody Olson, thank you. Is it true you concoct potions for the women to consume?"

A gasp blanketed the crowd.

She straightened her back and never batted an eye. "Potions, tinctures, brews... call them what you will, I make herbal remedies for my patients. Natural ingredients that assist them with ailments or help them along in their pregnancies. This I have done for ages. It is nothing new or secret."

"So, you can make a drink to help a headache?"

"Aye," she nodded. "I can also make a salve to calm to the fiery burn of a woman's parts after birth."

The Magistrate squirmed again but ignored the comment. "You can make a tea to stop cramps of the stomach?"

"Aye. I have a recipe for a girl's moon blood. It works quite well, although it doesn't taste very good," she joked as she eyed some of the younger girls in the front row. Some women nodded their heads in agreement.

"Who taught you these recipes?"

"My mother, and her mother before her, and her mother before her. I come from a long line of women's healers, of necessary midwives."

"Do you have a recipe that could cause the loss of an unborn child?"

Silence swept the room and Goody slowly turned her head to the side to stare the magistrate in the eyes. The magistrate quickly looked to Galen for help.

"Pardon me, Magistrate," Galen said. "I know I'm fairly new in New Haven, but it's my understanding that Goody Olson is a valued member of our community. Not once have I heard anyone speak ill of her or mumble of ill intentions. As far as I can tell, Goody Olson is revered, respected, and loved."

"Well, Reverend," the magistrate huffed, "because a community member is loved doesn't mean they are beyond reproach. I feel my line of questioning is..."

"Excuse me, Sir," Goody interrupted, "but am I being questioned on the murder of crows left at my doorstep or my medical practice? I feel your line of questioning seems to be veering into unchartered territory as I was led to believe my participation here was for other purposes."

"Yes, yes, Goody. I assure you this is all connected," he said, waving his hands around dismissively.

Margaret Fletcher shot up from her seat with a *thud*. The wooden bench grumbled from the release of her weight and bounced upon the floor. "She gave Winnie Gordon a drink!" she cried. "And now Winnie is without child! We all saw her miscarry shortly after ingesting the brew!" Winnie Gordon huffed next to her. She looked gaunt and disheveled with her lips pursed tightly in a wild sneer.

"Goody Fletcher, please sit back down!" the magistrate instructed. "Goody Olson," he continued, "is it possible that you miscalculated some of your ingredients?"

"Oh no," Goody Olson said, "I follow each recipe to the exact specifications. I've never misjudged."

"She has books! Tomes! Grimoires from the devil!" Goody Fletcher yelled.

The audience's murmur rose to a deafening din, and magistrate banged his gavel.

"Goody Olson has just testified that her knowledge has been passed down from the old country," Galen declared. "These books you speak of, while ancient they may be, are nothing more than recipe books from the last slivers of her family line."

From the corner of the room, Tansy rose from her seat. "What about the *Malleus Maleficarum?*" The room went silent again. "That's an ancient book," she said sheepishly. "I saw it in her home. I saw it on her shelf. She possesses it, or rather, it possesses her."

I shot Tansy a look of death, as if a thousand knives protruded from my eyes and pierced her heart. She winced, and I knew she felt it.

"Speak true, Goody," the magistrate demanded. "Do you have the *Malleus Maleficarum* on your shelf?"

"Aye," she said without pause or hesitation.

"The Devil book of Tituba?" he gasped.

"Aye. That is no secret, either. William Phips, the once Governor, is kin to me. After the folly of Salem, he entrusted it to me for safe keeping. I am the guardian of the tome so as not to allow it into the wrong hands."

"*You* are the wrong hands," Winnie Gordon growled.

"Sweet child, I promise you I've done you no wrong. I meant you no ill will," Goody said directly to Winnie.

Winnie threw her arms wildly in the air and stood up frantically. "You're a murderer! You're a liar! And you're a witch! Everyone here knows it! Everyone here whispers behind your back about the fantastical spells you impose, but no one speaks truth. Well, I speak truth! What you did to me! What you did to my baby, my poor, sweet baby!" She fell to the floor in crazed agony as Jedidiah reached down to help her back to her seat.

I raised my hand and the magistrate nodded for me to rise. "I've seen the book in Goody Olson's home as well. It was hidden on a shelf, it's a wonder I noticed it. She was very uneasy of my knowledge about its existence at first but was very forthcoming with how it came to be in her possession. It was just as she said. I have seen Goody Olson do great things. Aside from pulling most of us present into the world, I have seen her help many women in the community, myself included. She has been a pillar for my family, and I truly believe she is doing the Lord's work. The book means nothing to her. It was obvious to me that she was just holding onto it to uphold a promise she made. I believe with my whole heart that there is nothing nefarious going on here."

Winnie glared hard at me from the corner of her eye, but when I was finished and sat back down, she hung her head low in a shameful way.

Magistrate banged the gavel again as Galen raised his hand for silence so that he could say his closing statement. "Goody Olson is not on trial for her work. We cannot give credence to suppositions and hearsay. She has done no wrong. She has admitted the possession of the book, and what is a book? Mere words on a page. She should be regaled for helping to calm the fires of Salem. Let us not forget why we were gathered here in the first place. The oddities of the last month have given us cause for alarm. And I don't believe in demons and devils among us. Spirits are what we manifest. The cats, the goat, the crows, all works of the human hand."

Suddenly, a sharp pain worked its way in my abdomen, deep inside my vacant womb. I doubled over until it subsided. I looked at Galen with stricken fear, but when he nodded at me, I knew. I knew my womb was in fact not vacant after all. Impossible. But not.

"A very sad, and jealous, and despondent human hand. The work lends itself to an outsider, yet not. Possibly someone who feels like an outsider. Someone in our community who has felt afraid, and small, and like they didn't belong for quite some time."

The power behind Galen's words shook the room. I looked over to Winnie. Her head sank lower with each sentence he spoke.

"...wronged and shamed. This person begs to be noticed and derides others out of spite and jealousy. Deep down, they are miserable, unfulfilled, and so very, very alone."

Winnie threw her hands to her face and wept uncontrollably. Galen waved a hand in the air, and I subtly followed his lead to quicken and strengthen the power of his spell. No sooner had I done it, Winnie fell back to the floor on her knees in hysterics.

"It was I!" she cried into her hands and a collective gasp rose from the crowd. "I am the outsider! I am responsible for the cruel tableaus!"

Magistrate's face twisted in confusion as Jedidiah joined his wife on the floor. Tansy squealed at her friend's confession.

"Winnie! No!" Jedidiah begged in disbelief. "Say this isn't true!"

"I confess! I confess! I did the deed!"

Magistrate slammed the gavel with all his might. In a deep voice, he boomed, "Winifred Gordon, on basis of your confession, I give you to the custody of the New Haven Harbor prison guard where you will hereby stay to await your trial on the counts of giving false testimony against Eliza Olson and terrorizing the citizens of the community. Guard! Please escort Goody Gordon to her rightful cell."

Douglas made a move toward Winnie. She stood up with Jedidiah at her side, her face stained with tears. As Douglas approached her, a look of pure confusion darkened her face, as if she was coming out of a temporary trance and didn't know what was happening around her. "Jed?" she squealed like a frightened animal. "Jed? What are they doing?"

"It's fine, Winnie," he tried to coax. "We'll get this sorted out; I promise."

Douglas came up behind her and pinned her arms to her back. Her two sons huddled together in tears as they watched their mother being dragged to prison.

"Jed! Jed! Please don't let them take me! Please don't let them!"

My eyes pleaded with Galen. He knew my disdain for Winnie Gordon and my pleasure at her confession. But the confession was false. He knew it. I knew it. We had made that happen to put an end to the mounting hysteria engulfing the community.

Our spell.

The wails from her children broke my heart. *There must be a better way*, I said to him in my mind.

"Magistrate," Galen said, stopping Douglas in his tracks. "Perhaps there's a better way. Clearly, Goody Gordon is not well. Who knows the trauma she suffered from her loss? I know we want to be fair and just, but is it so fair and just to lock away a mother of two? Look to her sons. They weep for their mother. Maybe there's a more merciful path we can explore."

"I am an agent of the law, Reverend. I don't deal with mercy."

"Then why did you seek my counsel in this matter if not to exhibit such?"

The magistrate ran his hand down his long jaw. "And what might you suggest as a merciful punishment for this woman?"

Make her leave. I said in my head. *Send her away.*

"I... I can take her away," Jedidiah spoke out. "We'll leave for Lynn tonight. Her sister and her brother-by-law live there. They will gladly take us in and see she gets the help she needs."

Galen shrugged his shoulders. "See, sending her off to seek counsel from kin. A much more merciful alternative."

Magistrate interjected, "What about your lands, Jedidiah Gordon? Your home?"

I'll take them, I said again on the inside.

"The church. I'll leave them to the custody of the church."

"Alright, alright! It's settled then. Guard, see to it that the Gordon family are en route to Lynn by nightfall. As reparations for her wrongdoings, all property will now be turned over to the possession of the New Haven Harbor First Church of God under the care of Reverend Galen Gentry. Goody Olson, on behalf of the entire town, I bid you my sincerest apology for this whole mess. You are truly an upstanding member of our community and to shame you here today is a blight on us all. And now, can we please put this lunacy about witches and devils to rest!"

With a final bang of the gavel, the Meeting Hall was dismissed.

Chapter 12

Sunday, November 20th 1695
New Haven First Church of God
New Haven Harbor, Massachusetts
The Afternoon of the Full Moon

In the days following the confession and departure of Winnie Gordon and her family, the town of New Haven Harbor had been free of any unusual occurrence. No more tableaus, no more fear, no more talk of witchy things amongst the people. It was like things had been prior to the dark times in Salem—Goody Fletcher flounced about the market gossiping about her neighbors, the Harmon children continued with their mischief, Blacksmith Johnson complained of the weather to anyone and everyone who would listen, and all seemed right in our little section of the new world. The absence of terror since Winnie left further solidified her guilt on the matter, and that was enough to satisfy the most common of people.

But I wasn't a common person. I knew the truth about many things—one of them being the absolute innocence of the confessed woman. A part of my heart hurt for her. I often thought how she must feel to look in the mirror and feel absolutely and utterly confused at her situation. The despondency in her eyes when Jedidiah escorted her out of the Meeting Hall was sad too. Her mind must have split at that moment as she tried to reconcile the truth with the warped, false memories implanted there. Did she get flashes of the truth? Did the flashes hit her so hard that she wanted to scream and fight, and did she beg her husband to believe her innocence?

I hope so.

I hoped Winnie Gordon suffered a lifetime of confusion and despair as punishment for her years of snide comments toward me, her wicked smirking sneer, and her endless derision.

And so, life went on around me—and inside of me. My freshly cleansed womb now harbored a different kind of life—one that quickly grew and quickly changed me. It hadn't even been a fortnight since Galen brought me to his cottage by the sea, yet I could feel the presence of *something* stirring within me. When I lay awake at night, my insides twisted, and shifted, and *sang*—not songs with music and instruments and voices— they sang with images and dreams and a magnetic charge that pinned me to the bed but made every limb of my body tingle and feel as if it were rising in the air. Like I was detached from the physical world and communing with something larger than myself. I thoroughly enjoyed those moments and would purposefully retire to my room early most nights to feel that power surging to full capacity.

Some nights, Douglas had been a problem, and I was fearful that my refusal to perform my wifely duties would only be tolerated for so long. I knew he wouldn't accept my pregnant condition as an excuse for a lack of intimacy. Nevertheless, he was happy that I even was pregnant, a fact that I reminded him of often. It seemed to placate him for a little while, so I enjoyed it while it lasted.

Tansy proved to be another problem as well, but she was easy to ignore. She sulked in the corners of the church as we worked, and she made herself emotionally distant from me. I pretended not to notice and went about our daily routine as if nothing had happened.

After services that afternoon, Galen sauntered out from his chambers to the front part of the sanctuary where Tansy and I had been straightening up. "Tansy! Barbara!" he called. We stopped shuffling and sweeping and dusting and looked up at him. "I'm heading over to the old Gordon residence. The magistrate asked if I would look for some important papers for Jedidiah so that he could have them sent over to him in Lynn. When you're finished here, make sure the back door is closed tight. I'll see you both tomorrow."

Tansy and I nodded at him, and before he turned around to leave, he said, "Oh, Barbara, one last thing. Before you arrive tomorrow, please stop off at Goody Olson's. She has a salve for me."

Tansy put her hand on her hip and gave a little snigger. "A salve? For you? I thought Goody only treated the women."

Galen smiled wide and raised his right hand. A white cotton bandage was wrapped around his palm so that only his four fingers showed. "Well," he began, "Goody is a healer, and I figure if it's good for the ladies, it must be..." he paused to examine the dressing.

"You need to be more careful lighting your own fires," I said sarcastically.

He glared at me with a knowing look, and I blushed. I couldn't help it. The sight of his handsome face sent me erotic thoughts and images. Flashes of what we had done together mixed with the wants and desires of what we *could* do together. My ears burned red as I tried to conceal my lust. He tilted his head and raised his eyebrows, "Well, as caretaker of this establishment, isn't it your job to see that my chambers are always warm?"

My cheeks flushed hotter, so hot that it felt as if the skin was going to melt away from my face. "I am always at your disposal, Father," I said and looked away with mild embarrassment.

"Very well," he said. "Have a wonderful afternoon, ladies." He quickly left through the back entrance.

Tansy shifted and scuffed her shoes against the floor. I turned my head to her with a questioning look.

"I don't like the way he looks at you," she mumbled from the side of her mouth.

I narrowed my eyes in disbelief. "What? What do you mean?"

"You heard me. I don't like the way he looks at you. His eyes are..."

"Stop it! You're being such a silly girl."

"And I don't like the way he talks to you."

I huffed a bewildered sigh. "Now you're being utterly ridiculous..."

"I am not."

It was my turn to place my hands on my hips and slouch to one side. "How so? I don't understand."

"It's peculiar, Barbara. It's too... too... familiar, I guess. He speaks to you more of a friend than a priest holder."

"Reverend *is* my friend, though. We work very closely together. He's always been my counselor, my advisor."

"But it's in his voice. There's more there."

I turned my back to her to hide my facial expression. I didn't want her to see any glimmer or hint in my eyes that she was perhaps correct in her assumption. Because she was. I had known the reverend in the most secret and carnal of ways, and my heart pounded just at the very thought of the things I had done with him.

Will do with him.

"I don't know what you're talking about," I said. "I'm going to go home now." And I started for the back door.

"Winnie told me something when you were in Salem with the reverend."

I stopped in my tracks and slowly turned around. "Oh really? And what did the terrorizer have to say?"

Tansy lowered her head and cast her eyes to the floor, as if she were ashamed to repeat and betray the confidence told to her by her best friend.

"Go on! What did she say?" I urged, and my voice echoed through the church.

"Something weird happened to her. With the reverend. She had brought him some food that one day and... and... and something happened."

"With the reverend?" I asked, stupidly.

"Yes. She wasn't entirely clear because she said it all happened so fast, like a dream. But..." she paused, and I could tell she was choosing her words carefully, "he assaulted her. Sexually. She said he forced himself on her. Lifted her on to the altar and penetrated her with his..."

Wild anger coursed through me like a bolt of lightning shocking the tallest tree in the forest. Grisly images consumed me, as Winnie's face flashed in my head. But it wasn't truly Winnie, not all of her face. In some flashes she was missing a tongue as blood poured from her opened mouth. In another flash, there were two holes where her eye sockets had been, and she cried crimson. In another flash, one side of her face was completely torn away, revealing the bone structure of her jaw and the sinewy substance underneath.

I shook my head quickly from side to side to relieve myself of those thoughts, and with three steps, I leapt over to Tansy and grabbed her by the shoulders. I shook her hard and stared deep into her eyes. "Filth! Lies!" I screamed. "The next thing worse than an accusation of witchcraft is an accusation of assault. Especially by a shepherd to one of his flock. Do you understand me? Reverend Gentry is a man of the cloth, a man who is devoted to the Lord. He would never, ever, do any such thing." The words flowed from my mouth with such ease and grace and conviction that even I believed what I was saying. Tansy stared back at me—her hazel eyes pleading for the truth, but something in them knew the lie. "Besides, we all know what Winnie Gordon has done. She confessed her sins. So, is it not within the realm of possibility that she made that story up?"

"I... I suppose," Tansy stammered, not fully convinced.

"Winnie is ill. In her mind. She suffers from the affliction of madness, for which there is no cure, Tansy. She's gone. I imagine years of knowing her husband's perversions drove her to the edge."

"You don't know..." Tansy raged in protest.

"But I do know. Everyone knows. Make no mistake, Jedidiah Gordon is an adulterer to the highest degree. It makes sense that Winnie would have thoughts of the reverend. It's no secret he *is* nice to look at. To fantasize about..." I drifted away into my prior thoughts.

"Barbara!" Tansy scolded, snapping me back.

"Come on, sweet sister. Don't lie and tell me you haven't thought of him in that way as well. What woman in this town hasn't? Pray tell me, when did it become a crime to have private thoughts?"

"I suppose not," she answered meekly.

"Precisely. But it is a crime to accuse a holy man of sinning in the most perverted of ways. Slanderous words tear towns apart, Tansy."

"I wasn't going to tell anyone, not even my husband. I wasn't even going to tell you."

"Good. Now maybe you can wake up and stop being so morose."

"I know you and Winnie had your differences and say what you will about her and the horrible things she did, but she was still my best friend. That fact remains. Winnie was good to me. We confided in each other. Helped each other. Laughed with each other. And now she's gone. As if she was dead. It's hard to adjust, is all. And I know you know what I speak of. You too, lost a close friend."

Sarah...

We had ridden to Salem with the stable boy that day. The boy, Ethan Charles, wasn't interested in the witches like we were as much as he was interested in Sarah's woman parts. He rode us to the outskirts of the gallows and told us he would meet us back there when it was all over. Sarah and I were ecstatic as the area around us swarmed with people. There was a strange aura in the air that felt like a thousand eyes watching everything for miles. A crow cawed from the trees, and I remember telling Sarah it spoke to me. I don't know why I said that, but she giggled with excitement. I remembered Susannah Martin right before she dangled into the next world. She held a chain in her left hand—silver, with an oddly shaped pendant attached to it. And I stared at Susannah. Stared at her until she faded away. She smiled at me, and I smiled back. Her smile was like a warm embrace that stayed with me long after the crowds had dissipated. There was something so comforting in the ritual. Peaceful. Susannah looked as if she had accomplished something yet unspoken. I would never forget those moments. When the others hanging next to her struggled and bucked wildly against their ultimate fate, Susannah swayed with joy, and her eyes sang to me.

When she had been extinguished and her body fell limp, the necklace in her hand dropped to the ground. I wasn't the only one who noticed, for Sarah insisted we stay until no one else was around. When we were alone, she hurriedly scrambled beneath Susannah's feet and grabbed for the necklace. I couldn't help thinking that it belonged to me, but I wasn't about to take the happiness away from my dearest friend. "A souvenir!" Sarah gushed as she looped the silver chain with the strange pendant around her neck. "I shall always remember you, Susannah Martin, and this blue-sky day of your death!" I didn't need a necklace to remind me of that day for I knew those images would be burned in my memory for forever, but if having that treasure made Sarah feel good, who was I to say otherwise? But I'd have been a liar if I said I wasn't at least a tiny bit jealous.

Sarah had worn the necklace day and night, never taking it off. She would tuck it under her shirt so that it could touch her bare skin and be "close to her heart." And I had noticed a marked change in her demeanor and attitude during those days. She had become more confident, more forward, more arrogant. She was set to marry the cobbler's son, Ezekiel Blythe, but she boasted to me about her exploits with Ethan and how they talked about running away together to Salem. Before I could counsel her either way, she fell ill. A mysterious fever had taken root in her so deeply; she never recovered. I buried my best friend less than a fortnight after we sneaked away to Salem.

But it wasn't until that moment, standing with Tansy in the church, talking about the loss of our two dear friends, that I'd come to think of the pendant—the silver looping chain with the curious sideways ornament attached to the center. An ornament that resembled a silver eye. I couldn't help but think Susannah Martin meant to give it to me.

"I know, Tansy, I know," I finally said to her before leaving. There was so much more that I wanted to say, so many words of wisdom I could have dispensed, but I didn't have the will to stand there and bring comfort to her. After I said goodbye, I headed straight to the Hutchings residence in hopes of having a conversation with Sarah's mother. It had been many years since I had come that way, and shame rose in me that I had neglected to pay my respects to Sarah's parents. That shame was validated when Goody Hutchings saw me at the door. Never did her stern face break into a smile, yet she threw her arms around my neck and welcomed me inside.

"Barbara," she sighed tiredly. "As I live." She led me into the kitchen and poured me a cup of tea. In just three short years, which must have felt like a lifetime to her, Goody Hutchings had gone from a bright, jovial woman, to a shell of her former self. Her arms were rail thin, and her hair had completely grayed over, sure signs of her living agony.

Her apparent displeasure at my presence left me feeling uncomfortable, and I spoke quickly to hide my unease. "My apologies, Goody. I know it's been some time, and I know I should have come to visit sooner. It's just been…"

"Hard? I know. I live it every day. Shackled to the ghost of her. There is nothing worse than the mourning heart of a mother. I hope you never have to endure it. I wouldn't wish that on my worst of enemies."

I sipped my tea and bowed my head. "I can't bear to imagine. Sarah was like a sister to me."

"Yet, her grave remains undisturbed."

"I… I haven't had…" I stammered, taken off guard.

"I know, I know," she relented, throwing her hands in the air. "Life moves on for us all. All, but me."

I wrapped my hands around the mug, letting the heat of it warm my palms. "Goody, I'm here to ask a favor."

She raised her eyebrows in interest. "Oh?"

"Yes, ma'am. Sarah had a necklace. It was silver with a unique looking pendant."

"Yeah, what of it?" she asked, but there was a suspicious, almost accusatory tone in her voice.

"I know how much Sarah loved that necklace."

"It's an ugly thing," she spat. "Given to her by an ugly person. That Charles boy tempted her!"

"Oh," I said with fake surprise, "I didn't know."

"Don't speak false, Barbara Flynn. I know Sarah told you everything. And I know it all started the day you two rode with him to Salem. Ethan Charles made her unclean. Gave her gifts from the devil. Made her abandon her promise to her betrothed. And she died because of it all."

I lowered my head in sincerity. "I'm sorry, Goody."

"Nothing we can do about it now. So, what about this necklace?"

"I remember how much it meant to Sarah, and I was wondering if…"

Goody Hutchings moved over to one of the cupboards, opened the door, took out a wooden box, and handed it to me. She nodded her head for me to open it, and when I did, there was a handkerchief balled up inside. "Ugly thing," she repeated. "Don't know why she wore it all the time. Right until the day she…" She stopped and gasped as tears sprang to her eyes. "It's cursed," she whispered.

I pulled the handkerchief from the box and unraveled it to reveal the necklace within. I dangled it in front of my face, hypnotized by its shape and sparkle. The beauty of it washed over me, and it felt heavy in my hand, like a great weighted mass of power. I sighed. I hadn't forgotten, but I had.

"Goody," I began, still looking at the pendant before me, "I'm with child. I suspect it's a girl. I am asking if I can have this necklace so that I may give it to my daughter and tell her the stories of my dearest friend."

Goody tensed up. "That's fine by me," she said tersely. "But just know it will bring you nothing but misery. Sarah wore that hideous thing, and she died. Her father, so distraught by her death, carried it in his pocket every day after we buried her. Ten days later, he was dead. I put the damned thing in the ground, only to have the dog dig it up and carry it to his spot in the yard. Ten days later, he was dead. That thing is cursed."

"I don't believe in curses. I just want a memento to honor my friend."

She marched to where I was sitting and swiped the mug away from me. "Then take it and be gone with you."

I rose from the chair and nodded to her. "Thank you, Goody Hutchings. And again, I'm so very, very sorry. I'll see myself out."

I made my way to the front door, but before I stepped outside, I flung the necklace around my head and set the pendant gently on my chest. A shiver ran its way down my spine like a blanket engulfing me. A voice called out to me from somewhere dark and deep. "Winnie," it said, as if instructing me to do something, and I immediately knew where I had to go.

When I walked out, I stepped a little bit lighter, like there was no gravity in my gait. The air was cold, I knew it from the puffs of smoke that came from my breath, but it had no effect on me. The sun was starting to melt off the horizon, but the world looked as bright as the beaming of mid-day.

Chapter 13

Sunday, November 20th 1695
The Gordon Residence
New Haven Harbor, Massachusetts
The Night of the Full Moon

Darkness lay within the Gordon home like a family crypt—cavernous and still, and I tiptoed inside sneakily. Even with the light of the full moon shining brightly overhead, I knew I would not be seen. Once a place of laughter and life, the home stood now empty, devoid of any signs of a happy family present. Sad, really, to think that innocent children played here not too long ago. Children who loved their mother whole-heartedly and looked up to their father without the stain of gossip attached to him. I thought about my own children and how they would be. Would they love me unconditionally? Would they know their father—their real father?

Would they help me reshape the world and bring forth the New Eden?

I moved to the staircase and from the top of the hall, a candlelight flickered from within one of the rooms. Like a moth to the flame, it drew me in, and I glided my way quietly up the steps. Immediately, I could feel Galen's presence. It called me. Beckoned me. Pulled me closer to him by an unseen force. Of course, I surrendered to his power and will, for he was my husband in spirit and soul and body. He possessed the very essence of who I was. And the children who swam inside me bound us together in blood.

The door to the room at the top of the stairs was partially opened—Winnie and Jedidiah's master's chamber—and I gently pushed it open. Galen sat at the edge of the bed. He looked like a dark angel in his black priest's cloak surrounded by the stark white comforters. He smiled when I entered, and I floated over to him, my heart bursting with joy and desire at the sight of his devilishly handsome face. He extended his arms, and I obliged him with a warm embrace. I nuzzled my head in the crook of his neck and let the scent of him fill my nostrils as he snaked his arms around my back and placed a hand on the back of my neck. I pulled back from our hold, looked deeply into his eyes, and leaned in for a passionate kiss. At the first touch of our lips, I began to quiver. A surge of warmth rushed between my legs, and an uncontrollable desire swept me up in his lips, his mouth, his tongue. I pushed his shoulders forcefully onto the bed and straddled over his waist, clawing at his cloak, furiously trying to tear it away from him. He lifted my dress up over my head so that I was naked before him, and he delighted in my form. With one hand, he held one of my breasts in a firm but gentle grip, and with the other hand he pressed his thumb against my nether region searching for my crown jewel of pleasure. I squealed with enjoyment as he quickly pumped his finger against the outside areas of me, teasing me with every touch while never going inside. I galloped and grinded my upper body against him as if I were riding a horse, and the necklace bounced in rhythmic time against my chest.

When I heard a noise coming from the other side of the room, I froze. It was a low squeal, much like the one I emitted from pleasure, but there was nothing pleasurable sounding in it. I stopped wiggling on top of him and furrowed my brow. If someone had entered the room, or seen us together, I was fearful of the consequences. Without moving his head or body, Galen's eyes traveled to a spot over my shoulder. I swiveled my head around to see where his eyes were guiding me, and my heart nearly stopped in surprise.

For there, in the corner of the room, Winnie Gordon sat naked, bound to a wooden chair. Her hands were tied behind her back, legs splayed opened with her ankles wrapped to the legs of the chair with rawhide thongs. A white gag lay in between her teeth, and a crown of tangled thorns was placed atop her mass of blonde hair. Her eyes pleaded with me for help when I looked at her.

Stunned, I jumped from the bed and turned back to Galen. He sat up and smiled again.

I clutched the pendant at my chest in a panic. "What is she doing here?" I wailed. "Why is she here?"

Winnie moaned and tried to buck her upper body against her restraints.

"I thought you trusted me by now, Barbara," Galen said calmly. "Are you not happy with your gift?"

"Gift?"

"She's yours. She belongs to you, now. Do with her what thou wilt. She is your next steppingstone to greatness. The woods. The womb. The book. The moon. The sky. The blood. It's all connected. You've felt it, heard it, seen it. I've told you, Barbara, I've known you for lifetimes upon lifetimes. Endless is our connection. I've seen you do fantastic things... wondrous things... things that would make the holiest of saints bow in supplication. There is a tremendous force in you waiting to be cracked open, waiting for you to punch a hole in the world."

My eyes glazed over at the song of his words, and I swooned from their melody. Winnie stirred again in her chair, and I was released from my trance. "But you're my priest holder. My counsel. *You* guide *me*."

He chuckled. "Correct. I am just a servant put here to help your power come to fruition. A guide, yes. A partner, in some instances."

I placed a hand on my abdomen. "The Blood Brother and Sister."

"They are yours and yours alone. I was merely a catalyst to assist you in their creation."

I gasped in shock. Winnie cried out against her gag.

Galen rose from the bed and came closer to me. He put one arm around my waist and placed a hand over mine, against my stomach. "After everything you've seen? After everything I've shown you? After everything you've felt deep in your dreams and your soul? This..." he pressed down on my skin, "this frightens you?"

"No. Not frighten. It is not the children I am concerned with." My eyes traveled to Winnie. She knew too much—witnessed too much. If she ever brought this information to Tansy or Douglas or the Magistrate or...

"Abandon your worldly notions, Barbara," he said, reading my mind. "You are holding yourself back from your own ascension. Free yourself of your fears and the judging eyes of others. Like the nights we've spent together. That is the real you. The truth and the light and the way."

I nod my head in Winnie's direction. "And her?"

"I told you, she is yours. And in being yours, she is no one. No one who matters anymore."

The necklace felt heavy against my chest, but a warm sensation radiated from it and filled my entire body. I slipped from his grip. "Mine?" I whispered and walked over to examine Winnie. She was cold. Her milky white skin was riddled with hen-flesh racing up and down her arms and legs. There was shame and fear screaming from her frightened doe eyes and her puffy, tear-stained cheeks. I knelt in between her legs, mesmerized by her perfectly shaped secret area. Even amidst her terror and confusion and fear, its soft blonde hair glistened in the candlelight, readying itself for an eventual invasion. I placed my hands on her knees, softly crept them up her thighs, and grabbed at the folds of her lap—my fingers dangerously close to her honey. The muscles in her legs constricted at my touch as more hen-flesh bloomed in different parts of her body. She looked at me with a gaze of pure frenzy as a trickle of blood dripped down the side of her face from her crown of black thorns.

"Mine," I repeated, with a hint of mischief in my voice.

But I did not desire her in that way.

Not like my desire for Galen, or Blodwyn, or even Douglas once upon a time.

Suddenly, there was music filling my head. A low beating drum in the distance. Voices singing out in harmony through the trees. The wind thrashed against the side of the house, and it spoke to me. Lulled me. Soothed me into facing the reality that I had known in my heart the second I saw Winnie tied up in the corner.

I knew what I had to do.

I moved my hands from the inside of her thighs, up the meaty section of her stomach, to the voluptuous mounds of her breasts. Her pale pink nipples were like a second set of eyes staring out at me, and I wished them to shut! I wished them to stop looking at me! I squeezed them hard, clamped down on them with such a force that Winnie winced and cried. Slowly, my hands moved upward still—caressing the outline of her chest bones before stopping at her throat. I wrapped one hand around her divine neck and applied a gentle amount of pressure, just enough to make her squirm and squeal. Was that pleasurable for her? Did she delight in the twinge of pain? Did her honeypot drip with warmth at the prospect of her violation?

Before I could investigate my queries any further, Galen knelt behind me. His strong manhood pressed against the part of my leg where my backside met my upper thigh. He bent his head and kissed the back of my shoulder and neck while swooping underneath me on the other side and grabbing at my breast. I squeezed Winnie's throat a little tighter, and she wiggled against the pain. She tried to scream out, but her gag blocked her cries, but more so, the music in my head drowned out any audible sound from her. Galen continued to wriggle against my leg in rhythm to the music, and in measured time, I gave steady pulses to Winnie's esophagus with my thumbs, teasing her much like Galen did to my sex before. My eyes fluttered in the back of my head, and when they opened, Galen had placed a knife on the floor between my legs—the same ceremonial knife I had found in his cabin.

The music grew louder, and the full moon shone through the window casting its light on our spot in the corner of the room. "Don't cry," I said to Winnie. "There's no reason to cry anymore."

I reached for the knife, planted my free hand on Winnie's thigh, and bent forward slightly so that Galen could position himself and penetrate me. His first thrust took me by surprise, but immediately, my petals bloomed open and hungrily accepted the full depth and width of his manhood.

I clenched the hilt of the knife tightly as Galen drove himself deeper inside. In my waves of ecstasy, I pawed at Winnie's exposed body. She was tight and tense but locked in place. There was no escaping the passion taking place before her. The stream of her tears saturated her cheeks and the area below her neck, but I scarcely took notice of her pain as Galen's stabbing motions caused me to rise higher and higher like being lifted from the ground and propped up into the most pleasurable height of heaven. I was swept away in his movements, surrendered to every plunge—every deep and shallow and quick and slow plummet—until I was once again at the brink of my own release.

I bent forward even more in order to allow Galen even deeper access as I was greedy to feel all of him in me—everywhere and all over. The ridges of his member ground against my insides and the throbbing heartbeat of his sex filled me with a pleasure that I thought would make me crazy. I couldn't stand it. But I could. And I endured. And I reveled with wild and reckless abandon. I placed my head between Winnie's legs, my face to her crevice. And even though I truly had no desire for her or her woman parts, I inhaled her, breathing in her intoxicating sweetness. Before I even knew what I was doing, I licked her there, tasted and savored her honey, taking her into my mouth and lapping at her like a lioness cleaning her young. I couldn't help myself. I had no intention of doing so, but I just couldn't stop myself from indulging. She wiggled hard against my tongue with quick thrusts as if she were guiding my mouth to find her outer pearl. When I did, I stayed there for some time, rolling the thick padded meat of my tongue against her sensitive nub. She moaned beneath her muzzle but cried harder in embarrassment. How confused she must have been as her whole upper body rocked with the sobs of shame, while her lower body rocked with the waves of pleasure.

Galen's pace quickened, and as I lifted my head from Winnie's lap, I noticed she was watching him with a wide-eyed, lustful stare. Enraged at her arrogance and nearing my own ecstatic release, I let out a guttural cry and swept the blade across her throat. The knife cut her through with a hiss and her blood spurted out like a font. Winnie made a gurgling sound in her chest as her life force drained from her. It covered me—drenched my face and chest and entered my mouth like sticky syrup. I lowered myself farther still so her blood could soak Galen, as well. When it hit his flesh, he plunged in me one final time as we both came to fruition.

Bathed in blood.

He exited me and lay in the red puddle on the wooden floor. Even though he had just relieved his seed into me, his organ was still hard and stood erect. I licked the blood from my lips at the thought of him mounting me again.

Winnie's head bobbled backward as the final drops of life fizzled in spurts from her wound. I walked behind her and removed the crown of thorns from her head.

"Mine, too?" I asked.

Galen looked up and over to me and nodded. I dug the head piece into my scalp and felt a line of my own blood ooze down the sides of my temples.

"Blood Witch of the Red Thorn," he said. "My Blodheksa."

I stood over him as he lay in Winnie's blood pool. His face and neck were stained crimson, and his manhood was still curiously fierce and ready. I dripped in Winnie's blood from my face to my stomach, but I also dripped with something else. My desire rose swiftly again, and there was an unnerving need for me to possess him again, to be part of him again, to be joined with him for forever until the New Eden took over the world. Slowly, I lowered my body down on top of Galen's, and he was in me once more—two twisted and bloodied bodies, united as one.

But our union was short lived.

I barely had a chance at a second swoon because, before I knew it, a figure was silhouetted in the threshold.

"Barbara?" the figure called in despair, disbelief, disgust.

The voice belonged to Tansy. How much she had seen, I could not know, but I did know this was not good.

"B... B... Barbara," her voice cried, the sobs of fright hitching in her throat. "Barbara, what's going on?" She was frozen in the doorway, trying to survey the scene.

I tried to release myself from Galen so that I could usher her out of the room and give her some crooked explanation, but Galen grabbed my hips and plunged me back onto him. He jabbed me hard on the inside and I howled from the pain. "No!" he ordered.

My face twisted. "Let me go! Release yourself from me!" I fought again, this time harder, trying desperately to confront my sister.

"No!" he repeated and forcefully drove himself deeper, and again I winced.

Tansy took a slow step in. "What have you done?" she exclaimed. "What is all this?" She walked about the room gingerly, her mind trying to take stock of the images before her. When she gazed upon Winnie's naked, lifeless body in the chair, her eyes went wild with terror. "You lie with the beast!" she screamed. "You lie with devils! You *are* devils!" She fell to the floor in frenzied hysterics.

Galen reached his hand up and grabbed at the pendant about my neck. I followed his lead, and he released his grip, leaving me with the ornament in my clutches. "Tansy, go home," I sternly commanded. "Everything is fine. I cut myself on the roses."

Tansy continued her wails.

Galen moved gently inside me, easing my fury and fear. "Tansy," I said again, calmly this time. "It's fine. Please, go home. John is worried about you. You got lost in the dark."

As if in a trance, Tansy rose from the floor. Her eyes glazed over as she looked at me, past me, through me. She was there, but she wasn't. I let go of the necklace. "I got lost," she said serenely, in a faraway voice. "But I'm better now." An eerie smile bloomed on her face, she walked out, and Galen and I finished our blood-stained dance.

Chapter 14

Wednesday, June 6th 1696
New Haven First Church of God
New Haven Harbor, Massachusetts
The Afternoon of the Waxing Crescent Moon

I had grown. Expanded. Four feet kicked me from within on a regular basis. Four fists punched and fought, eager to escape their watery cocoon. I begged and pleaded with them to stay inside for as long as they could to maintain the illusion we had established. They listened as best as they could, but that didn't stop their assault on my insides. Ribs, abdomen, intestines, bladder—they cared not where their strikes landed. Each night, I rubbed them down and spoke gently to them, and when I closed my eyes, I could hear them giggling to each other, speaking quickly in a language only they could understand. It pleased me so to carry this miracle around, even as the weight of them felt massive as the summer months had begun to dawn on us.

The winter months, on the other hand, had been especially cold and dreary, and if I had to guess, I don't think the sun had appeared for at least forty consecutive days or more at one point. A gray gloomy sky was a permanent fixture during that time, and it blanketed every man, woman, and child's heart with a somber feeling of mourning and depression. "The worst winter in forty years," the elders had proclaimed. The gray wouldn't have been so bad if not for the cold that accompanied it. Any other given year would see the children enthusiastically playing after a snowfall—building all types of snow creatures on their front lawns, lying down and swishing their arms up and down to create snow angels, and annoying Goody Fletcher by organizing snowball war counsels in her back yard (because everyone knew the Fletchers had the most spacious property). But not this winter—this last winter brought isolation and fear. The people opted to stay in, stay warm, and stay safe.

Be that as it may, my work continued at the church alongside Galen during that time. I maintained the pretense of loving and dutiful housewife by day, but by night was a different story. Galen had taken possession of the Gordon home under the guise that it would eventually be used as a community outreach center—one that the world had never seen before! He had laid out his master plan to the congregation, promising them that the property would be washed away of its sin and put to good use for the benefit of our town. There, he would put into place a program for the children, the younger generation. He knew that going to weekly sermons was tedious for the teenagers to endure, so he wanted to create a place for them to gather, talk about their faith, and learn about each other and the world on their terms, at their level. It was brilliant! He had said the purpose was to make it fun and exciting, to keep them interested in God and their faith as children, so they were rooted more strongly in their faith as adults. Who could argue with that? Galen also proposed that the upstairs quarters be converted into temporary housing for emergency situations. He did not want to see any of his flock suffer, so if there was a crisis at hand, and a person, or family, found themselves in a dire situation where they would need a place to stay, the home would be used as a provisional shelter. Galen received much praise and adoration for this proposal, but what truly became of the Gordon house was another story, for that was where Galen and I came together and carried out our clandestine affair.

So, the days were spent working at the church doing my usual duties, but as far as Douglas was concerned, there were nights when Reverend needed assistance with planning the particulars of the Gordon house project. As long as I was home at a decent hour and didn't neglect my responsibilities at home, Douglas was content with the arrangement.

However, Galen's true vision didn't involve the community at all. Many nights, we gave in to our carnal cravings. I indulged in him, and he in me, with reckless abandon. We submitted to the most primal of desires—performing ungodly acts that suited our every whim and pleasure. But some nights, we lay in Winnie's bed where we gently held each other and mused about the life growing inside me. He would nuzzle his face to my bulging stomach and hum songs to the children. They would turn over and kick wildly at the sound of his soothing voice. Some nights, we read from the *Blodheksa* book, and he would tell me stories of long ago, of the things he'd seen, of the lives he'd lived. I was especially entranced with the stories involving me, for it was often hard to reconcile my prior existences with my present life. Most nights felt like a dream—like a cold and dark dream that I wished to never wake from. But some nights... some nights were deathly silent, and we spoke only through our minds. Those were the most chilling of nights because I wasn't present in the real world. When I read his thoughts, heard them, saw the words in my mind's eye, I was in a trance that detached my spirit from my body and lifted me to a different realm. Galen said it was much too dangerous to do that very often as I ran the risk of getting lost, or even worse, having my body possessed with a placeholder spirit and never being allowed to return.

Tansy found out that she, too, was with child. The happiness on my mother's face when she learned she would be a grandmother but twice in one year was enough to drive a person sick with sweetness. Tansy glowed at the news, and her husband, John, proclaimed to his circle of friends that he had the strongest seed in New Haven Harbor. Goody Olson said it was lucky for two sisters to be pregnant at the same time, but it didn't feel so. Since the night of Tansy's discovery of Galen and me, I had had to maintain the glamour spell I placed upon her. And remembering what Galen said: *A glamour is only a mask. A parlor trick. But it's temporary*, I knew I would have to tread carefully when in Tansy's presence and be cognizant of my words and actions to not retrigger her memory. The medallion around my neck preserved the glamour and served as an essential tool in keeping the truth to what Tansy saw at bay. Even so, Tansy wasn't the same after that night. She walked around as if she were in a foggy daze—as if she were being compelled to exist by some outside force. I knew it was because of me, because of what I had done to her. I almost felt bad that I had to possess my dear sister in such a way, but the result otherwise would have been death for my children and me, and their protection was paramount. I had no choice. The pendant I so faithfully wore was my solid defense in keeping my secret safe, and every time I saw Tansy, I repeated the words in my head over, and over, and over.

However, there was a valid explanation for Tansy's aloofness—one that did not raise suspicion of an otherworldly nature. Word had been sent from Lynn that Winnie Gordon had

gone missing. Jedidiah said that in a fit of madness, and after much arguing and pleading with
her, she had taken off into the night and never
returned. She was presumed dead. At the news of
her best friend's disappearance, it was no wonder
that Tansy became despondent and standoffish.
But I knew the truth, and Galen knew the truth,
and Tansy, somewhere in her hazy mind, knew
the truth. And I knew there would be no body to
ever be found. Winnie Gordon no longer existed
in this life or the next.

Wednesday afternoons were when Galen
called the small service. It was usually a handful
of the community members who gathered for an
informal prayer or two, some fellowship, town
updates and other types of conversation. Now
that the weather had turned and the sun had
warmed the land, we convened on the back lawn
after praying inside. The wooden chairs were situ-
ated in a circle, and after Galen had led the group
in prayer, we sat chatting and laughing about
trivial things. Tansy walked around the circle
filling our cups with lemonade. I had offered to
help—as church hand, that was part of my obli-
gation, but she smiled weakly and told me to stay
seated, that I looked like I needed a break. She
was right. The Blood Brother and Blood Sister had
been especially rambunctious all morning, so I
nodded and thanked her for the reprieve.

I leaned back in the chair and raised my face
to the sky. The hot sun beat down upon my face
as a line of beaded sweat sprouted at the top of

my forehead. I sighed heavily, and my entire upper body heaved deftly in place. "Goodness! Look at you!" my mother exclaimed in joy.

Douglas laughed. "She's barely making it up the stairs these days!" I shot him a nasty look, for I couldn't stand it when he spoke about me as if I weren't there. Galen noticed and shook his head at me, as if to warn me of my facial expressions. I huffed a little knowing laugh, and the others in the circle assumed I was agreeing with my jokester husband. It was all very comical.

Douglas laid a hand on my stomach and rubbed the top of my protrusion furiously. The children swatted at him from the inside, upset that he had come so close. I knew they didn't like him as they would often stir and fight at the mere sound of his voice. "This little guy is a fighter, isn't he?" he proclaimed.

I nodded and did my best to force a smile as the circle chuckled. "Every time I'm in the room, every time I talk to him, he bounces and moves around like I've never seen!"

I grabbed his hand and removed it from my abdomen. "Yes, yes," I said, "and the nausea takes root in *me*. You get the enjoyment of the outside motion, but for me it's something else."

The women in the circle hemmed and hawed knowingly; the ones who'd experienced the heaviness of the end of a pregnancy nodded in agreement. Their faces were haunted with the memory of their own changing bodies, their own trials with bringing life into this world. It was something only a woman could empathize with. Yet, it was the perfect excuse to be rid of Douglas's touch and settle the children down at the same time.

"You wait," I called to Tansy. "You'll have your day soon enough!" Again, the women chuckled with their nostalgia. Tansy looked my way, but her expression was dark and cold. She filled the last cup belonging to Marcus Watson and shuffled with the pitcher back inside the church.

"What will you call him?" my mother asked a moment later. "Have you decided?"

I looked at Douglas, and his face went blank. "We haven't really discussed it. I mean, I was thinking we would see him first and then decide on something."

"But there has to be a name or two that you're more inclined toward," Goody Fletcher said. "And what if it's a girl?"

"Oh no!" Douglas defended with certainty. "It is definitely a boy!"

"William," my mother declared. "William is a fine name."

"For my father and brother," I said, and I thought I saw a tear roll down my father's cheek.

"Douglas? After yourself?" Goody Sheare suggested.

"No, no!" Douglas protested. "I am the only Douglas Flynn this community can handle."

"Gabriel? Gabriel is strong and pious," Goody Fletcher said.

Douglas cocked his head to the side. "I like Gabriel. That was one of my uncle's names."

"John?" Tansy's husband said with a snicker.

"I fancy you would like that name for your own son," I teased, dismissing the suggestion.

"You're ignoring the other half!" Goody Jones called out.

Douglas waved his hands in the air. "She can call it whatever she likes if it's a girl!" It was the men's turn to laugh.

"What about Trent?" Galen said, and the circle went silent. "For the River Trent in the mother land. It means 'he who brings the flood.'"

My ears perked up, and I smiled. Douglas crinkled his nose and stuck out his tongue. "Oh no! That's a terrible name! A foreign name!"

"Trent Flynn has a nice ring to it," I spoke out.

"Nope. Nope," Douglas insisted. "David. He will be David. That is my judgment."

"To David!" Goody Fletcher said raising her cup.

"To David!" the congregation responded in unity.

But before I could reluctantly put my cup to my lips, the children kicked me hard on the inside, and a stream of water seeped into my lap. A stream of water that was certainly not from my cup but from the inside of me. The children were letting me know it was time. A stabbing pain doubled me over, and my cup fell to the ground. "Oh woman!" Douglas bemoaned. "Look at the mess you've…"

Chapter 14

But after I howled in pain, my mother immediately jumped up and shouted, "The baby!"

Within moments, the congregation had surrounded me, while Douglas remained in his seat, dumbfounded. Galen was instantly by my side, lifting me up to my feet. "Run!" he commanded Douglas. "Get Goody Olson immediately."

"But it's not time!" he said, dumbly. "There's still time left!"

He was right. Had I still been with his child, there would have been one more moon cycle to go. Technically, there should have been two moon cycles for the children, but I knew they were not of this world and would not conform to the laws and physics of men.

"Which is why there could be trouble!" Goody Fletcher yelled. "Go, Douglas! Now!"

Sweet of her, I thought. But I knew there would be no trouble.

My father took me on my other side, and he and Galen helped guide me into Galen's chambers and laid me on his bed. *How odd*, I thought to myself, *this is where I lost life, and this is where I will bring life to the world.*

My mother shooed the congregation away, as Tansy hurriedly prepared for Goody Olson to have the tools necessary to usher my children into the world. Mother bid Galen to leave, but I insisted he stay, giving some thinly veiled excuse as to why I needed him. Mother obliged, and Galen knelt beside me and held my hand. He stared at me with his soft gray eyes and spoke to me with his silent voice. He told me it was time, told me to be strong, told me I was the most beautiful woman bestowing the most beautiful gift upon the world. I smiled through the pain.

"What do we do if Goody doesn't get here in time?" Tansy asked my mother.

"This is Barbara's first child. It should take a while. I have no doubt that Goody will be where she has to be when Barbara needs her most."

The contractions and pressure in my abdomen told another story. "I'm not so sure about that," I said.

My mother's face twisted. She pulled up my dress and bent my knees up so she could inspect my situation. Her eyes went wide. "Well," she sighed, "I've had five children of my own and witnessed numerous births. I suppose this is my time to bring one in. Breathe in deeply, my love. The baby is coming. Tansy, I will most certainly need your assistance at this time."

I didn't labor for very long, for by the time Douglas returned to the church with Goody Olson, I was resting comfortably in Galen's bed with two bundles nestled into the crook of each arm. "What happened?" Douglas exclaimed breathlessly. "The baby is here? Goody is too late?"

Goody raised an eyebrow at my mother and joked, "Ahhh, Goody Wilkins! Looking to take over my position, I see."

Mother smiled and gave a soft laugh.

"Babies," I corrected, and Douglas's face fell to the floor.

"Which explains why they were early," Tansy chimed.

"Oh yes," Goody Olson added. "Not enough room for the two of them! Let me have a look!" She came to me and the babes and examined them quickly. "Healthy as far as I can tell." She then lifted the blankets to assess my level of trauma, and she was satisfied with what she saw and proceeded to clean the bed and the room.

Galen stood in the corner like a stone sentry guarding his realm. I knew he wouldn't speak to me until my family left.

"Shouldn't Douglas come see them?" Tansy asked dryly.

"Oh yes, of course, of course," I replied with mock excitement. "Come Douglas, come see."

Douglas awkwardly lumbered to the right side of the bed, while Tansy stayed next to me at my left.

I gently lifted both my arms so that he could get a better look. "This is David, your son," I said, tilting my right arm. "And this is Gretchen, your daughter," I said, tilting my left.

He bent forward a little closer and smoothed back the bundling from each of their faces. Their sweet little eyes were closed, and they were happily dreaming.

"They weren't this calm but fifteen minutes ago!" my mother gushed.

Tansy shifted and huffed. "Barbara!" she whined. "Give him one! Let him hold one of the babies!" Agitated, she leaned her body over and snatched David from my grip. As she pulled him from me, my hair that had been a tangled mass underneath the babe's body, snagged in his bundling. My necklace had also been twisted in my hair, and as she pulled, the metal clasp snapped, and the chain fell between my breasts. When David was safely in Tansy's arms, she pulled back and stared at me. The fog from her hazel eyes collapsed and she looked at me wild, confused, and afraid, as if she had just awakened from some horrible nightmare. I looked to Galen in the corner and terror overcame the both of us. David began to cry, and Tansy clutched him close to her chest. "I… I…" she started to say, but Douglas walked over to her and cumbersomely removed the boy from her arms. He went on babbling about something as David proceeded to scream.

Tansy snapped her head to Galen, then back to me.

She *remembered*.

I knew she remembered.

She knew I knew she remembered.

Without a word, she fled from the church, and I feared for what was to come.

Chapter 15

Sunday, June 10th 1696
Reverend Gentry's Chambers
New Haven Harbor, Massachusetts
The Night of the Waxing Gibbous Moon

I had given birth in Galen's chambers and that is where I remained for a few days. Galen suggested I stay there rather than move the children and me back to my own home. It would have been an unnecessary and strenuous trek he had said, so he let me stay where I was comfortable for a little bit. During the day, my mother would come to the church. She lit candles, made sure the windows were open and closed when they needed to be, fed me, and of course, doted over her beautiful grandchildren. My father stayed away most of the time, as he felt it wasn't his place to be involved in maternal affairs. "I'll see them when I see them," he grumbled, and that was fine with me. Douglas usually visited quickly before he went to the Jail House for the day and would stop by again on his way home. And Galen was with us the entire day. He told everyone he was staying at the Gordon Residence during the nights, but in reality, he never left our sides.

Goody Olson also would come to check on us. Since the children had been born a tad prematurely, she said she wanted to keep somewhat of a close eye on them to be sure. But I knew there was no need for that. David and Gretchen were perfect in every way. They had strong, healthy, perfectly pink little bodies with shocks of white atop their little heads. When they cried, they mewed like kittens—it was an animalistic sound not of this human world. It sounded as if they belonged somewhere else, somewhere in the woods, somewhere where they could sprint and leap and play. "Not yet, little ones," I said to them with a chuckle. "They'll be plenty of time for roaming this Earth!"

I learned quickly that they didn't like to feed individually, so I endured the daunting task of having them both at my breasts. When they latched on, they would touch their hands together and stare up at me with their dark blue eyes. Once, they gripped me so tightly, they both drew blood. I screamed out from the pain of it, causing them to suckle harder. But their faces! Their sweet, angelic faces as they drew the blood and milk into their tiny mouths eased any pain my physical body bore. Often, I would get lost in the depths of their ocean-colored eyes, and I would smile and sing and talk to them. They were smart. Advanced. It amazed me to see how they persevered to lift their heads and coo at me on their second day of life! And immediately, they took to their names and followed me with their eyes when I spoke. I bonded with them the instant they were placed in my arms. Pure energy made flesh. I had never felt such deep love for another person in my entire life.

The nights, however, were the most magical times, for that was when *they* spoke to *me*. Their voices sang out to me in my dreams, singing to me the most beautiful and ancient songs. They sent visions to my brain, and the three of us were completely connected to each other in mind, body, and soul—three individuals working in concert with each other. I told Galen about the vivid dreams and the music I heard in my sleep. He smiled and said, "They remember. They remember everything. When a child is conceived, they have all the knowledge of the universe inside of them, but when they are born, the trauma of birth is so impactful, they forget everything when the pain of life rocks them to the core. Your children are different, Barbara. They still remember. Listen to them, for they will only remember for a fraction of time. Learn from them, for they teach you the old ways until it is time for you to teach them."

I swept back their hair. "The knowledge of the universe locked away in these perfect little heads." And I kissed them both.

To say I was in complete awe of them would be an understatement. Douglas, on the other hand, was less than impressed. "What's wrong with their hair? Why do they have blue eyes? We both have brown eyes. Shouldn't they have brown eyes too? Why do they scream so loudly?" Those were his common complaints. My mother explained it away as his inexperience with handling children, but I knew the truth. David and Gretchen flinched at his touch, squirmed when he held them, cried when they heard his voice. And I didn't bother to ease the situation or tell the children they needed to put on their disguise for their foster father or give Douglas some words of encouragement or comfort when dealing with them. I didn't care. They were mine. Not his. And he no longer mattered in the equation.

Overall, the days spent in the church were days of pure joy. I wished I could stay there, with them, like that, forever. But the time came when Douglas insisted I return home and get settled in our normal routine. Neither Galen nor I could argue as we knew there was still a ruse to maintain.

Douglas left the Jail House earlier than usual that day. He came to the church to get me, and we rode back to our house. The twins were swaddled in their fleece blankets, and I held tightly to the both of them as we bounced in the Constable's carriage. My heart sank as I approached the front door, for the longing I had for my church bed blanketed my entire being. I knew this house wouldn't do. I knew this place wouldn't suffice. I knew the children wouldn't grow and flourish within these walls. But I sighed and resigned to enter, resigned to the next few years of glamouring the people around me and waiting for the moment to be whole with the children.

David and Gretchen both tensed up as I walked inside. "Easy now," I tried to coax them, but they simultaneously fussed in my arms. Immediately, my senses piqued. Their distress was disturbing, and I knew they were sensing something off, something not right. I soon got my answer when I was met with the stern faces of Tansy, Goody Fletcher, and Magistrate John Williams in the parlor.

I twisted my head to Douglas, who had entered the home behind me. "Wha... what's all this?" I tried to say nonchalantly as I brought David and Gretchen closer to my chest.

"Go in, Barbara," he said. "You need to hear what they have to say."

Slowly, I walked in, but I kept a safe distance from them. The children wriggled. "Goody. Tansy. Magistrate," I said, acknowledging them. "By the looks of things, I surmise this isn't a homecoming. Would someone mind explaining why you all have graced my home with your presence?"

Tansy dipped her hand into her pinafore pocket and pulled out a book. My book. My heart stopped beating when she dangled *Blodheksa* from her forefinger and thumb. Her nose crinkled in disgust as she held the book in front of her at arms-length. "This! What is this?" she chastised.

I adjusted the babies in my arms and said nothing.

"I found *that* is your closet," Douglas continued. "Your mother asked me to bring you one of your dresses while you were convalescing at the church. And lo and behold, there it was, on your closet floor." He was lying. I knew I had hidden the book away very well. He only found it because he was snooping. So why did Goody Olson tell me only I could see it? Maybe it had something to do with my broken necklace...

Tansy fanned the pages out and tossed it onto the end table.

"What does this even mean?" he asked. "What does this even say? It's symbols and runes and ... and scribbles of madness!"

"A book for a witch!" Tansy shouted, and Goody Fletcher clutched her chest. Gretchen made a small whimper, and I bounced on one hip to calm her down.

"I've examined the book, Barbara," Magistrate said with a heavy sigh. "It does look rather odd. Suspicious."

"Would you care to explain the meaning of all this?" Goody Fletcher interjected.

"We're at a moment in time where an explanation is in serious order," the magistrate added. "I already brought this to Goody Olson. She wasn't very forthcoming when I questioned her knowledge of this text. I was not satisfied with her ambiguous answers. Douglas escorted her to the cell this morning, and she awaits further questioning."

My head swam. "You put Goody Olson in a cell?" I spat at Douglas. He lowered his head in shame. "Questioning about what? Speak forward with me!"

"No, Barbara, you're the one who needs to speak true," Douglas said. "These are very serious accusations..."

I opened my mouth to try to defend myself against this ambush, but nothing came out. If only I could have reached down into my pocket and clutched the eye of the broken chain. If only I could concentrate on the voices and faces in front of me and not have to calm the wailing babes...

"Accusations?" I was finally able to say. "I haven't heard any accusations from any of your mouths! Just an inquiry on some strange book found in my closet! For what am I being accused?"

"Reverend Boone," Goody Fletcher blurted. "You wouldn't let anyone see him that day. We all asked where he was, and you made excuse after excuse, and then when we finally pressed you to check on him, he was dead."

I furrowed my brow. "Are you insinuating that I had something to do with Reverend Boone's passing?" I roared in disbelief. "That is the most preposterous thing I've ever heard!"

"You have to admit, it doesn't look right, Barbara," Douglas chimed in.

"Reverend was an old man! I loved him like a grandfather. I would have never done anything to harm him! This is madness!"

"And then the tableaus that appeared right after Reverend Boone's death," Goody continued.

"Magistrate and Reverend both passed sentence on Winnie Gordon for those crimes. She confessed to those sins! We were all present in the Meeting Hall that day when she threw herself to the floor and admitted her transgressions!" I defended.

Tansy's eyes went wild, and she pointed a finger at me. A calm rage washed over her countenance, and she tilted her head slightly forward. The shadows of the candlelight darkened the circles beneath her eyes, giving her a wicked look. "Then you killed her," she said flatly.

Goody Fletcher gasped.

"Excuse me?" I shot back at Tansy.

Startled by this new allegation, Magistrate rushed to Tansy's side and put an arm around her shoulder. "What do you mean by this, Temperance?" he said gently.

"I saw," she said in a trance-like state, as if the scene were replaying in her mind's eye at that very moment. "I saw the grisly tableau, although it wasn't a tableau, it was the reality. Winnie's neck was sliced open like a sow to the slaughter. And I saw it. I saw Barbara. She was mounted over the beast, and he thrust himself into her with his ungodly organ. His cloven hooves smeared in Winnie's blood! His horns tapped a rhythm on the floor as she bucked against him, but I saw him! Horns and hooves and tail and teeth! I saw his misshapen and gnarled body violate my sister, and she moaned with pleasure. You enjoyed it, didn't you? You enjoyed the company of the beast like all witches do!" Tears sprang to her eyes as her voice quavered. "She lay with the devil!" she finally declared. "I saw it with my own two eyes! She lay with the devil and those children are the spawn of Satan!"

"They aren't right, are they?" Goody Fletcher observed in accordance with Tansy.

"Devils," Tansy whispered as the venom dripped from her tongue. I grasped the children tighter as real fear began to creep its way into my bones. They cried, louder, fiercer.

"That sound!" Goody exclaimed. "Why, that's not the sound of crying children at all!"

Silence swept over the room, and my heart sank again at the severity of her words. I knew I needed to leave immediately, get to Galen, and get to safety, for the only true devils in my company were the ones before me. And they didn't wish me well.

I turned and made a move to exit the front door. I needed to run as fast as I could, away from this group of hateful, accusatory people.

Douglas shifted his body to block my path. "They're not mine, are they?" he asked, but it was more a statement begging for confirmation and not a real question.

David and Gretchen let out another ear-piercing wail against my chest. "Step aside, sir," I said in a low, firm voice.

"Forgive me, Barbara, but I can't."

Soon, the four of them surrounded me. Tansy and Goody each snatched a baby from my arms, and their deafening cries filled the room. Magistrate pulled my arms behind my back as I tried to reach desperately for my children. "Tansy! Stop! Margaret! Please! Give them back to me!" I howled frantically.

"Barbara Flynn," Magistrate said behind me, "as Magistrate of New Haven Harbor, I feel there is enough evidence to conduct a formal trial for the accusations brought forth against you. You are hereby remanded to the custody of Douglas Flynn and the Constable of the City and will await your review and trial date."

"Douglas!" I screamed. "I beg you! Stop this!"

Perhaps I was too weak, too depleted from childbirth. Perhaps the breaking of my chain and the revelation of my book served as a spiritual detriment—for whatever I said, whatever gestures I used to aid in my escape and retrieval of my children, did not prove fruitful. I was utterly powerless and utterly alone.

"David! Gretchen!" I called out for the twins. "Douglas! Listen to me. They're merely babes! Days old. They need their mother. They will starve without me. They will die without me!"

I thrashed wildly against the magistrate's hold as he shoved me out the door and back into the carriage, saying: "And in the case of David and Gretchen Flynn, the children will await sentencing while in the care of their aunt and father.

They will endure the tests to determine if they are, in fact, the spawn of the Prince of Darkness."

Tests? I knew of all the tests they performed on the accused witches in Salem, and to think they would do any of that to my sweet babies filled me with murderous rage. The drownings, the pin pricks, the touch tests, the bodily exams... the thought of hands on my children, prying and prodding for marks of the devil, threw me into complete hysteria.

"I curse thee, Douglas Flynn!" I screamed as he readied the horse to lead me to the Jail House. "May you suffer an eternity of flames for this sickening display of malice against your wife and children! I curse thee, John Williams! May any hand that touches my innocents fall from its wrist! I curse thee, Margaret Fletcher! May the wailing cries of my children fill your head both day and night, driving you to take your own life! And I curse thee, Temperance Foster! May your betrayal and false accusations strangle you and your unborn child in your sleep!"

They stood on the porch as the carriage rode away, and I stared them down with eyes of fury. My children's cries echoed in the air and stayed with me until we reached the Jail House.

Chapter 16

Sunday, June 10th 1696
The New Gaol Jail House
New Haven Harbor, Massachusetts
The Night of the Waxing Gibbous Moon

"Go, Barbara! Stop fighting me and get in!" Douglas exclaimed as he shoved me into the small cell. I thrashed against his grip as best as I could, but I knew the inevitable. He shut the door behind me, and a feeling of dread came over me. The room was black as pitch, save for a ray of light creeping in through the circular hole in the wall—the one the jailers used to check in on the prisoners without having to open their wooden doors with the metal reinforcements. I was never one to fear the dark—in fact, I reveled in it, embraced it, made love to the nighttime, but this? This was a different kind of dark. This was the dark of loneliness and despair. This was the dark of death. This was the dark of an inescapable void. It filled me with terror, and I tried to breathe in deeply to catch my despondent breath.

Douglas stared at me through the view hole in the wall, and defensively, I eyed him right back, but I was in his domain, his territory. He ran the Jail House that had been so affectionately called "New Gaol." Six years ago, over in Barnstable, they called their Jail House "Old Gaol," so, of course, in New Haven Harbor fashion, there was a desire and need to comply with what was deemed "Massachusetts Legacy." Thus, New Gaol was built as an almost exact replica. The wooden structure was exactly like a house, so as to not give the impression that anything bad or wrong happened here. But in truth, it was a place to hold people waiting for their punishments to be doled out. Whippings, walks of atonement, and public floggings were all part of the bargain. But New Haven was a relatively peaceful town, and it was a rare occasion to have serious criminals in our midst. Our one claim to fame was that we had avoided public execution at all costs. Not one person in the history of New Haven Harbor had ever been put to the gallows. Yet, as I laid my hands upon the reinforced wooden door of my cage, I had a strong feeling that was about to change.

"Douglas," I begged through the peephole. "Tell Reverend Gentry to come see me. Tell him what's happened. I need his guidance and spiritual counsel."

"That's not possible. The Magistrate has determined that you shall have no visitors while you await your trial." Douglas took a small step back and came into full view. His pleading eyes were pathetic to behold, and a small voice creaked out of his throat, "Why?" In that instant, I was overcome with such rage and disgust at the sight of him that I hissed and spit at him through the hole. A cackling laughter rose from the cell next to mine, emboldening me to do it again. So, I did. A second time. He wiped my sticky saliva away from the side of his cheek, shook his head, and walked away. The ray of light left with him. My heart sank at the thought of Galen being barred from me.

I had recognized the owner of the echoing laughter almost immediately. Goody Olson was my neighbor in this wooden cell. I put my lips to the opening in the wall and called out, "Goody? Goody Olson is that you?"

In an instant, there was a knocking from the other side of the wall and a rustling from within. I envisioned her cell was just as dark as mine and she was trying to maneuver herself to the circular cutout in *her* wall. "Good evening, Barbara!" she sang, and her voice indicated she was not in distress.

"Goody!" I exclaimed. "Are you alright? Why on earth did they put you in here?"

She sighed, and it filled the entire floor. "You know they've been glaring at me with their suspicious eyes for quite some time now, child. And no matter how much good you do in the world, the only things anyone ever seems to remember are the mistakes. I am well, dear. I knew this day was upon me eventually. It was foretold to me many, many moons ago. A lifetime ago. It was only a matter of time. Which is fine. I've been waiting. Outstayed my welcome, I suppose. Long ago, someone very close to me had warned me of this day."

"Hush, Goody! Don't say such things! Lest someone listens to us at this very moment!"

"Let them," she answered resignedly. "There's no use in hiding anything now. They had my fate decided a very long time ago. But don't you worry, child. Those who strike against me will be met with certain judgment."

Pain struck me deep in my heart and burst out of my eyes in tears. "But you're so critical to the survival of this community. How can they treat you like this? This isn't fair," I sobbed, but it wasn't just the matter of the old woman's imprisonment—I had much to sob over. My chest was heavy with the absence of my children and the uncertainty of their fates. My chest was heavy with the betrayal and scorn from my sweet sister. My chest was heavy with my own failures that could have easily been avoided.

"Cry not," Goody said. "Failures can always be rectified to successes. I've seen so many of them, Barbara, you wouldn't even believe!"

My breath hitched in a small gasp. Had she read my deepest, despondent thoughts? Soon, she was knocking on her wall again, so I moved slowly to my side of the room opposite the noise. She drummed against the wood methodically with a measured, heartbeat-like rhythm. I pictured, in my mind's eye, her gnarled fingers curled into a fist and her knobby knuckles rap, rap, rapping on the hard gray wood.

Thump, thump, thump.

In rhythmic time, the sound created a song—deep and soothing. It lulled me, called to me, calmed me. I pressed my hand to the wall and felt the *thump, thump, thump* reverberate against my palm and spread up my arm and into my chest and down my core. I closed my eyes, and when I did, I was no longer in the cell—no longer shut away in a wooden cage. I was in the clearing of the Black Wood Forest, in my special place, underneath the light of the full moon. The trees swayed and danced as the music continued to *thump, thump, thump.* A red glow blanketed the horizon, and a soft fog haze lifted from beyond the trees. My eyes started to sting and water, and I soon realized it wasn't fog; it was a thin layer of smoke spiraling up in the distance. The acrid smell lightly filled my lungs, and I breathed it in happily. But the light of the moon bathed me, illuminated my naked body, and pulled me in a frenetic dance to the sound of the heartbeat drum. My own heartbeat aligned in time with the rhythm, and I swayed. And I swayed. And I swayed. Like the gentle bowing and wavering of the silver trees. I was swept away in it. Lost in it. A voice called to me from deep in the wood—a guttural voice of the ancients from yonder guiding me to look to the sky. When I tilted my head, it was there—the tear, the rip, the stars that had shifted to form an opening so great and wondrous. From down below in the clearing, it appeared to be the shape of a woman's sacred parts and I thought: *what shall the sky birth tonight?*

But the music corrected me immediately. The ripple was not a means of bringing forth some new form of life, but rather it was a gateway, an entrance to somewhere else, somewhere chaotic, and glowing and gruesome and beautiful all at once. The voice told me to enter the gateway, but it was the sky, and I was firmly planted on the ground. I became confused, and upset, and lost as the need inside of me to punch through the sky rose higher and higher.

The red glow approached closer, and the smoke became denser. The trees danced and bowed their limbs even deeper so, heavy with the weight of a hundred bodies hanging from ropes tied tightly around their necks. There were faces that were familiar to me—Martha Corey, Sarah Good, Rebecca Nurse, Susannah Martin, Goody Olson. But there were also the distended faces of those whom I did not know—faces I had never known, and yet I had borne witness to in my dreams and visions. White-haired girls, and black-haired girls, and faceless men with gouged out eyes, and long-haired boys with the devil in their eyes and "X's" burned deep into their foreheads. All their swinging bodies dragged the limbs of the trees closer to the ground.

Soon, I was joined by two children—a boy and a girl, pale-faced and black-haired. They must have been around eight or nine years old. The boy reached for my left hand, the girl for my right, just as they were when I held them last. They couldn't be David and Gretchen, but yet somehow, they were. They clasped their free hands together, and the three of us went dancing in a circle, skipping to the heartbeat drum, breathing in the encroaching smoke, and laughing under the moonlight.

There was gritty ash on the ground, at our feet, and I stopped dancing for a moment to bend down and touch it. It was fresh. Hot. Ashes of the bodies and trees burned in the forest. I pressed my hands to the ash, driving my palms deep in the pile, grinding them into the dirt, and mashing the ash and bone fragments into the pits and grooves of my palms. The children watched me and did the same. At once, we raised our hands to our faces and pressed them against our cheeks.

We carry the dead with us, I thought.

"We always will," Goody Olson's voice broke into my vision. She was not with me in the circle, but she was with me. Somewhere. "I was the Blodheksa once, until I wasn't. And I have spent an eternity searching for my kin. It was always you."

Her last words echoed in the forest and in my head, and I suddenly opened my eyes. Met with the darkness of the cell, I stared out for a while until I finally fell asleep.

Friday, June 15th 1696
The New Gaol Jail House
New Haven Harbor, Massachusetts
The Afternoon/Night of the Full Moon

When Douglas came to me to bring me something to eat, I begged him to let me go. He refused, of course, so I proceeded to beg for him to at least let me see the children. I was worried for their health and safety. If he would just bring them to me so that I could feed them and hold them, but alas, that was another fruitless request. He told me they were being minded by Tansy, and that Goody Sheare's niece, Hester Wallace, had recently given birth and was acting as a wet nurse for the twins.

"A council from Salem has arrived to assist the magistrate in his evaluation of the babies," he added through the hole.

"And what kind of evaluation would that be?" I growled behind gritted teeth.

"You know, Barbara," he sighed. "Please don't pretend you don't know."

I pressed my hands to the walls and gripped the opening with two fingers as if trying to claw my way out of the cell. "Please! Douglas! Don't let them do anything to them. They're innocent. They're good. They're pure."

"Magistrate said the children would not be subject to lawful scrutiny if only you confess."

"Confess? Confess to what?"

"Confess to the acts of witchcraft and spell work. Confess to possessing a book to guide you in devilish acts."

Goody Olson shuffled in her cell. My desperation got the best of me, and the walls and the darkness made me feel small. I thought if I gave him something, anything, my request to see David and Gretchen would be honored. I pounded my fist upon the wood. "Alright!" I screamed. "I confess! The stupid book is mine!"

Douglas took a step back and I saw more of his figure from behind the hole. He wrung his hands nervously together in a defensive stance. "Reveal its origins. From whence did it come?" he pressed. "What role does Goody Olson have to play in all of this?"

"None," I lied. "I found the text hidden deep in the woods."

Douglas went silent for a few moments, and I watched him walk over to Goody's cell wall, peek through her wall hole, then back to face me.

"Douglas, please. I told you what I wanted to hear. Now please let me see the children, if just for an hour."

"Magistrate said the children would not be subject to lawful scrutiny if only you confess."

"But I did! I just confessed to my knowledge and possession of the *Blodheksa* book."

"Confess to the murder of Reverend Boone or at least your involvement in his untimely death..."

"Untimely death?" I scoffed. "He was but a thousand moons!"

"Confess to the murder of Winifred Gordon..."

"Are you serious, Douglas? A murder with no motive, no weapon, no body..."

"Confess to your adulterous relations with the Prince of Darkness, the beast, the Unholy One..."

"As reported by whom? My deranged sister? Where's the proof in that!? Speculation. Conjecture! Slander! Embellish!"

"Confess the children were not fathered by me."

I paused. My mouth closed tight with a gulp, and we stared at each other through the small space of the hole. He shook his head, bewildered, and left the cell.

"They will taint the Wallace woman, you know," Goody Olson said some time after Douglas had left.

"What do you mean?" I asked.

"The children. They are not meant to suckle from anyone but you, their mother. Lord knows the effect your children will have on Goody Wallace, and Goody Wallace's son who is still on the breast as well. Their essence will surely produce some reaction in them all."

"Hmmm," I pondered. "Positive or negative?"

"Most certainly a negative one," she replied.

"Negative how?"

"It's hard to say." She sighed. "But I am sure of it. At least for the young boy. An infection will grip him and take root acutely inside. And the longer he shares the teat with the Blodbrødre and

Blodsøster, the more his senses will dull, and his heart will darken, and he will grow monstrous in spirit and misshapen in soul. He will bring shame and misery to those closest to him."

"Good," I said flatly. "Let them all suffer."

Hours later, Douglas returned and the door to Goody's cell flung wide. "Thank the Lord!" I cried. "Thank you, Douglas. Thank you for letting her Goody go."

But a silence filled me with fear again. "They're not letting me go, child," Goody said in a strong, confident voice. "I suspect the gallows is where I'm headed. Fear not, my dear. I go before you always. I have lived out my days tenfold. The hour is near."

There was no reply from my husband.

Frantically, I pounded on the walls. "No! No! You can't do this! I confessed! I confessed! Goody has nothing to do with this! Nothing!" I screamed, and flailed, and slammed my hands against the hard wood until the skin of my palms shredded open, smearing the timber with my blood. And then a thought overcame me, something I hadn't considered before. I had been so wrapped up and despondent over my children being taken away from me that I hadn't realized that Galen was still on the outside. He could help me. He could help the children. I had had no visitors during my incarceration and had assumed the magistrate had forbidden it until my trial, but this was a dire circumstance. "Wait! Wait! Get the reverend! Get Reverend Gentry. He is my closest confidante.

He will vouch for me. He will at least vouch for Goody Olson! This treatment goes against the laws of God and men, Douglas! You know it! Get the reverend! Please!"

I watched through the peephole. Douglas had Goody's arms restrained behind her back, and he slowly turned his head in my direction. "The reverend's gone, Barbara. He fled the day I brought you here. No one has seen or heard from him since."

My heart and body sank to the floor, and I wept uncontrollably in the darkness. I lay there, motionless and numb, for what felt like an eternity. There was no reprieve from the stifling summer heat in this tight, windowless cell, and it made it all the harder to breathe. He left me? He left without saying goodbye? He abandoned me in my most dire time of need? Why? Why would he forsake me now?

I tried to imagine the clearing in the forest. Tried to imagine again the scene I saw when Goody Olson tapped her fingers against the wall. But I couldn't. I couldn't go there or transcend mentally and spiritually from my cell because softly in the distance, babies cried. My babies.

David and Gretchen.

And a raucous tumult rose from the back yard of the New Gaol. Voices carried in the summer air. A strong presence gathered beyond the walls. Cries and shouts and hoots and hollers. Animal sounds masked as human voices. I pressed my ear to the wall to try to hear them better, but it was futile. Muffled. Drowned. But I knew what they were saying wasn't anything good. I heard someone speak Goody Olson's name, and the crowd roared. I smelled fire. Smoke. Rising higher. Screams. Goody Olson's screams. The crowd roared again. Flames crackled louder until she stopped wailing. The stench of burnt flesh carried through the night and in between the slats of this poorly built house. They executed her. They sacrificed her! My stomach turned, and a blanket of red descended over my eyes. I pounded on the walls again, full fist punches, desperate to escape.

The cries of the babies grew closer. More distinct. Clearer.

"Abominations!" someone yelled.

"Spawn of Satan!" another howled.

"Let them be cleansed!" a voice screamed.

I pounded harder, more furiously, as if to tear the wall down, to tear the jail down, to tear the faces off every man, woman, and child in that crowd!

But I froze when David and Gretchen shrieked in unison as the flames licked at their tiny bodies. I think my mind detached from myself when I heard their pitiful mews of pain and anguish. The flames roared again, and the crowd roared again, and the fires consumed the lives of my precious babes.

Chapter 17

1696, day unknown
The New Gaol Jail House
New Haven Harbor, Massachusetts

Time ceased in that instant. I slid to the floor when the screams and shrieks rose to the highest crescendo then fell to a hushed whisper. I heard them all as my body trembled, and I stared into the blackness of the cell. There was no more time, no more blackness, no more cell, no more me. In my weakened state, I descended into a void of nothingness, collapsed upon myself, and withdrew into my mind. I left this earthly plane. Forgot everything, everyone, everywhere. Simultaneously, there was nothing and all. Numb. And I gave myself to the feeling—handed my body and soul and mind and heart as offerings to the great beyond. The Great Unknown. For I wanted nothing more of this earthly existence. With the atrocities of the human world blocked from any acknowledgment, I was able to step outside of myself, dip my toes in the great beyond, and *become*.

There was comfort in the darkness. Every time I breathed it deeply into my lungs, every time I let it wash over my body, it was like the first time I had ever taken a breath. A newborn babe being born over, and over, and over again. The darkness was tinged with the acrid scent of smoke, and I welcomed that in as well. The poison shook me and awakened the darkest parts of my being. I was transformed in that cell. In that darkness. In that black night solitude. There were no guides left to assist me—no Goodys or Galens or children or Witch's eye medallions or books. It was me, and me alone. The darkness summoned me to gather my strength, to pull from that ancient part of me that still existed at my core. The ancient me who had manifested back through time.

And once I did, I could see for miles!

I saw the span of time that coursed through the universe like the veins in the human body. Ribbons of highways made from thousands of stars. I wanted to reach out and touch them all! And there were hundreds of gaps—ripples of stars that tore open hundreds of sections in the sky. Each one led to a different moment, a different world, a different dimension. I saw moments from the past that struck me as strange. Primordial rituals with altars, and animals, and runes and dancing. I could have danced with my ancestor witches for eternity! There was a simplicity in their worship.

I also saw moments in the future that confused me. Great machines beyond my comprehension dominated the land, yet the sentiment remained the same. I was drawn hundreds of years forward to a black-haired girl levitating in the sky. The light surrounding her was magnanimous, and she dreamed of forests and burning and smoke and blood. She was also on her journey as our paths crossed. I reached my hand out to grasp for her, but she was a fraction from my reach. *Be not afraid. I go before you always...* I sang out to her the words that Goody Olson said to me, but I can't be sure if she heard them or not. I was drawn to her darkness, like it was familiar, like I had seen it before. *She smells like Gretchen.* But I knew she wasn't her. *Princess Joephie Gretchen Bluebell Thorne,* a child's voice echoed in the night.

"You are the nothing," an ancient voice said. "You are the everything. You are the darkness." I struggled to reach for her, to stay with her, to teach her everything I knew and learn all her secrets at the same time. But her path led her elsewhere. She had other undertakings to complete before she could make her impact on the world. I pulled back my arm knowing I should no longer interfere with her assignment. She had much to do and to endure. I briefly saw her own confinement of sorts and couldn't help but think that even after centuries had passed, the persecution of my kin was alive and well. Something barred me from advancing forward. The tear in the sky faded and closed, and I saw my spirit sister no more.

After that, the images I saw in the beyond were emblazoned into my mind and onto the fringes of forever, for I had a true understanding of the purpose of the nature of things: there must always be a Blodheksa. The Blodheksa brings forth a sacrifice, an offering. The Blodheksa then shapes into being the Blood Brother and Blood Sister. Together, the three, the Unholy Trinity can garner tremendous power, the likes of which the world has never seen.

How long my vision quest lasted, I cannot say, but I was replenished with a new sense of strength and purpose. It could have been minutes. It could have been days. It could have been months. I was none the wiser. But when I returned, I was disoriented and confused and couldn't remember the bulk of the events that had transpired.

My eyes blinked rapidly as Douglas snapped his fingers in my face. Slowly, his visage came into focus, and I was able to see him more clearly. "Are you back now?" he inquired with surprise.

I responded with a small moan, and my brain scrambled to fit the pieces together. Images from my vision quest were still fresh and vivid, but the reality of my physical existence was making its way back to me.

He sat back onto the floor from his kneeled position and relaxed his shoulders against the wall. I looked about the cell and saw a tray of food set beside me. He gave a long sigh of relief. "I thought we lost you there!"

I tilted my neck from side to side letting the stiff bones pop and crack. I tried to create some distance between us, so I curled my knees to my chest and hugged my folded legs.

"What... what happened?" I said in a daze.

He reached his hand, touched the top of my foot, and frowned. "I've had to take care of you this entire time. It's been a struggle, and we all prayed you would pull through. And now you're back. And we will make things right again."

"Make things right again?"

He tilted his head forward and lowered his voice. "I'm sorry, Barbara. You know it had to be done. There was no other alternative."

I cocked my head and furrowed my brow. "No other alternative?"

He moved his hand from my foot to my face and swept a lock of my hair from my eyes. When his fingers wavered by my nostrils, my muscles tightened, and my eyes went dark. A surge of energy jolted throughout me. I had to clench my jaw to restrain myself—to subdue the rage that shocked my veins.

It didn't take long for the confusion to fade away, for I remembered everything.

"Your hands smell like smoke," I said flatly.

He brought his fingers to his face and gave a whiff, and his eyes shifted nervously when he smelled it. "The Constable and I were cleaning out back. It's been a while. Things needed to get back in order."

I closed my eyes and thought about the fire. I thought about Goody Olson screaming. I thought about the babies smoldering from innocent pink to black and bone. Their sweet faces contorted as their flesh melted away into oblivion. I thought about it so clearly, so vividly, that soon, I opened my mind just wide enough so that the fire blazed within me, consuming the very essence of my being.

"Barbara, the magistrate will pardon you. No harm will come to you. Confess your sins, admit your transgressions, and all will be forgiven. The land has been cleansed of the true beasts. Their souls washed clean of any evil and sin. If you are humble and brave, and display true sorrow in your heart, the magistrate will allow you to live in repentance."

I gave no reply, and Douglas pulled back with fright when I finally looked at him again. His face washed white with deathly fear, and he hurried to his feet and stammered, "H… h… how is it…"

Did he see what I felt?

Did he see the flames in my eyes? Did he feel the heat rising from my body? Did he smell the stench of the burning ends of my hair as I stood up to meet him face to face?

I was on him in a second. My hands wrapped around his throat as I shoved him back against the wall. He was stunned, frozen, unable to defend himself for I acted so quickly and without warning.

And I was on fire!

Every ounce of preternatural energy that coursed through me was pure fire. My blood boiled within. And I pressed upon him with a deathly grip that closed off his airways. He gurgled and thrashed and tried to free himself of my hold, but his motions only increased my power over him. And I smiled! I smiled when his eyes went wide with terror, knowing these were his final moments. I smiled when his eyes bulged from their sockets and blood rimmed their corners. I smiled when I smelled him start to burn and his skin sizzle and singe. My fingers left a black, charred ring around his throat. And when I had finally seared his gullet closed, and he could no longer draw breath, he went limp in my hands, and I released his lifeless body with a *thud* to the floor.

I marched over him with a long striding step, walked out of my cell, and up the back steps to the side door of the Jail House. I was the only prisoner who was being held there at that time, so there were no witnesses to my actions. Not that I cared. There would soon be no witnesses to anything anymore...

The sky was completely blue without a hint of clouds to be seen. A cool breeze blew from the east, and I inhaled the fresh air hungrily. I had been deprived of it for so long that it added another layer of energy to my already charged self. However, my heightened senses detected the soft undertones of smoke in the atmosphere. I walked down the side staircase and out to the back of the

Jail House to where the crowd had gathered and cheered during my children's demise.

Just as Douglas had said, much had been cleaned and cleared away, but there were still remnants of the massacre left behind. There was a circle burnt in the grass—burnt all the way down into the earth so that ashes of wood and fragments of bone were embedded deep in the roots and the soil. I knelt before it on my hands and knees and wept into the circle. I breathed in the burnt embers and caressed the sides of my cheeks in the grass. I wanted to feel the very last remains of my children as close to me as possible. And I crumbled. I crumbled into a pile of my own ash and dust on the inside, as I felt that weak, helpless sensation invading my psyche again.

Be not afraid... I heard Goody's voice call to me from somewhere far away, yet somewhere so close by. *Keep your good thoughts flowing...* Galen's words came back to me. *You are the darkness...*

As if on instinct, I scooped up the ashes from the ground and filled my apron pockets with them. They took my children away, but they could never *really* take them away, I thought. Soon, I heard the Constable's voice approaching, and I knew if I stayed any longer, I would be found, so I absconded to the only place I felt safe and at peace ... the clearing in the Black Wood Forest.

It truly was a perfect summer day. The woods teemed with the sounds of life—the glorious singing of the birds and the twittering of the squirrels. And even deeper, so deep down in the depths of the soil, the ants marched, and the other creepy crawlies muddled about. I heard it all! It filled me so, and I clutched the outsides of my pockets, drawing David and Gretchen ever so close to me, and I danced around with them in a circle. We held hands and sang songs, and we laughed and laughed! There was music from beyond the forest, and the trees joined us in our dance. "Oh David! Oh Gretchen! We are so blessed to be here in the Black Wood together enjoying this most splendid day!" I exclaimed, and I whirled them around, lifting their shadowy bodies from the ground, rising them higher and higher into the sky.

So high until they were gone.

Vanished.

Released from my grip and no more.

I looked around for them frantically. "David! Gretchen!" I cried to the trees. "Where are you, my little ones?" The trees shifted and bowed. A long silver limb dipped forward and pointed at me, and I suddenly remembered that yes, they hadn't gone anywhere. They were with me. In my apron pocket. Disintegrated to dust.

Slowly the rage returned. It smoldered. It burned.

Smoke rose from the ground around me in thin billowy puffs, and the heat that I had experienced in my body when I'd extinguished the light from Douglas's eyes was now back in full force. I looked down to my palm, and tiny sparks released from my fingertips. I planted my feet firmly into the grass and threw back my head to the summer sky.

Dark clouds gathered overhead, and I raised my arms, lifted my voice, and called to the great beyond. I screamed the words of the ancients—the words from the Blodheksa line that had been passed down to me. But it was always me.

I was the Blodheksa, until I wasn't.

I thought of David.

I thought of Gretchen.

I thought of how those horrid people had doused away their precious lives—how they extinguished their fires before they had a chance to set the world ablaze alongside me. I lived among a town of monsters. They were real. They were dangerous. They stole my future from me and needed to atone.

Thou shalt not suffer a monster to live!

When the blaze reached a fever-pitch height within me, I opened my palms and wailed. I pledged myself to the oblivion, and the dark one, and the great beyond, and the legacy of the Blodheksa. Affirmation of what had already lain dormant in my soul from the moment of my birth. Affirmation in concrete words that I was now an acolyte of the dark, baptized in thorns, and forever dedicated to the coming of the New Eden.

I released. I released all the fiery energy from my core. And soon enough, in the distance of the Black Wood, in the heart of New Haven Harbor, a low panicked din rose above the forest and an acrid smell wafted in the summer breeze. One by one, the homes and stores were set aflame. And the fires crackled. And the people screamed. And their bodies burned helplessly in their homes. The scent of burnt flesh filled my nostrils—the flesh of the animals in the barns and the people flailing in the streets. All of them. Monsters. Disintegrated and piled up into heaps of ashes and bone, only there would be no one to scoop them up and carry them forever.

Something exploded in the distance as the sky rumbled with a low growling thunder. My parents. Incinerated. Another explosion trembled the ground, and the clouds gathered darker. Tansy. John. Smothered. Gone. Returned to the dirt. And Goody Sheare, and Goody Fletcher, and the Hansons, and the Wallaces, and the Meeting Hall, and the Gordon Residence, and the Flynn Residence, and the New Haven First Church of God, and the General Store, and the School House, and the New Gaol. All of them Monsters. Reduced to cinders.

Ashes to ashes...

When the sky burst open and the summer storm was upon me, I knew it was my time to leave. I clutched my apron, clutched the ashes of my children, and walked away from the ruin of what was once New Haven Harbor.

Chapter 18

1696, day unknown
Location Unknown
Somewhere in Massachusetts
Night of the Full Moon

I had walked away from the Black Wood Forest and from the ruins of New Haven Harbor. I had walked away from the destruction and decimation. I left it all behind me and wandered. Through daytime and heat and darkness and wilderness and rain and cold—I roamed the terrain aimlessly. I hid among the shadows, passing through town after town. Sometimes someone would see me, and I would work up the strength to glamour myself into invisibility. Sometimes I wouldn't care and allowed the kindness of strangers to feed me, or put me up for the night or let me wash up in their bath houses. Once, a sweet woman saw my shoes were so worn down that my little toe was sticking out the side, so she gave me a fresh, new pair. "You are too kind," I had said to her. "And your kindness will surely be the death of you." She went white with fear at my words. I can't remember if she lived through the night. I soon became a pox—for everywhere I went, every town I ventured through, chaos and death followed, and I dared not stay in one place too long for fear of suspicion, accusation, and reprisal. So, I carried on with my children safely in my pockets as my own power recuperated, swelled, and coursed through my body.

The moon cycled at least three times during my journey, and when the air began to shift and turn, I knew winter would be creeping upon me soon. And as I ventured among the trees and sleepy communities, the stench of the New Haven Harbor incineration stayed on me like an impossible stain. No matter how many lakes and streams I washed in, no matter how many baths I took in strangers' homes, the smell was always there to remind me of my triumph. And the song of their dying screams stayed in my ears like an immutable sound. It was there in the daytime when I meandered in the valleys. It was there in the evening when the crickets chirped their insect symphonies. Like a hymn being lifted to the Lord on high. And if I listened close enough, I could pick out the individual voice of each individual monster and replay their suffering again and again in my mind. What a glorious feeling it was to hear Goody Fletcher scream as she melted to nothing! What a giddy rush that overcame me to hear Magistrate's hair sizzling on his head!

As my power replenished, I could envision the twins ever so clearly. Sometimes they were seven years old with dark skin and heads of curly black hair. Gretchen had amber eyes and David had gray—like fire and ice. Sometimes they were sixteen years old with pale skin like the driven snow, and their eyes blazed wild with a purple glint. Their silver hair poked out from the sides of their black hooded robes, and ancient runes were tattooed in black on their forearms. Sometimes they were five years old with China-blue eyes and pin-straight blonde hair. Sometimes they had my face—my brown eyes and brown hair, my button nose, and oversized lips. Sometimes they had Galen's face with his wide grin and stormy gray eyes. Sometimes they bore not the face of human design and were but stone and rock and stars and branches. And sometimes they were just shadows—billowing smoke rushing through the treetops and swirling around me in a playful dance. Regardless of the iteration, they were always *them*—Gretchen and David, David and Gretchen. And no matter the form they took, no matter what version of them they revealed to me, I was content to just be in their preternatural presence. They filled me with a happiness only a mother could know. They told me stories, sang me songs, played games with me, and most importantly, taught me the ways of time. I absorbed their lessons and teachings hungrily, even when I didn't fully understand the language or the words. I tried hard to remember every detail of the dreams and visions they imparted on me, for I knew they would be helpful to me in the future.

Chapter 18

One thing was constant—I kept moving. Walking. Wandering. I knew not where I was headed, but I knew once I got there, I would be at home. And while the company of my little ones was satisfying and filled me with great joy, I started to long for the company of a human companion. My thoughts soon turned to Galen, my priestly demon lover, and the ache in my loins grew ever so painfully. He was the lock to my treasure chest! When I was with him, I felt free and unconfined to the shackles of the mortal coil. He amplified all power within me! When we were together, we were unstoppable—a force to surely be reckoned with. Together, I knew we could ascend. Together, I had no doubt that the New Eden I had read so much about could become a reality. But he had left me. And as much as that pained and confused me, I surmised it was the only way to protect us. I had to believe that was the reason, for any other excuse would have pained me beyond that which I could handle.

And then it happened! One night as I lay in a haystack of a foreign barn, Galen appeared to me in my dream. His dark hair was swept to the side and his gray eyes smiled at me. There was a storm brewing on the horizon of his eyes, and lightning crashed down in them as he laughed. He was devilishly dashing in his reverend's cloak, and when I approached him to open it up, I was met with his throbbing manhood in full sight. It had been so long since I had touched him, smelt him, tasted him, and felt him way down in the depths of my own body! I quickened and jolted at the sight of him and his naked glory. In an instant, I was on my knees, running my hands up the sides of his thighs and savoring the way his flesh felt against my hands. I twirled the little hairs on his legs between my fingertips as I rose closer to the insides of his groin. He moaned, and the familiar sound excited me so and sprang me into action. With one hand, I gently cupped his stones, and with the other, I pulled the skin of his shaft in a jerking motion before taking him fully into my mouth. But like most dreams twist and turn without warning, I no sooner had the full length and girth of him at the back of my throat when the scene suddenly changed. I was still on my knees, but Galen had oddly disappeared. In his stead was Blodwyn! The visionary lover from Galen's cottage! The one he had proclaimed was actually me! She stood with her legs spread before me, and the silver tuft of her sex at my nose. I placed my hands on her hips and tilted my head back so that I could look up at her. She was just as I remembered—her voluptuous breasts bounced heavily at her upper torso, and her white hair dangled at her sides. Without further hesitation, I pressed my lips to her nether region...

...and woke up.

But upon rising from slumber, I knew what needed to be done.

I needed to get to Galen's cottage in the woods—the place he took me to that unlocked all my inner secrets, the place where I reconciled all the apprehensions of my true nature and gave myself to the powers of the dark. It was the place where the children were conceived under the cold moonlight and the stars shifted to form the opened mouth of the sky. That was home. That was where I needed to be. Under the cover of darkness, I left the barn and set out to find it. I knew not where it was, but I knew how to find it.

David held my right hand and Gretchen my left, but they chose to remain in their shadow forms as we traversed across the land. The closer we got to our destination, the quieter they became. I knew they didn't want their chatter to prevent me from hearing the directions of the moon and the stars and the sea because, as we approached the secret area of the wood, the lapping of the water against the rocks on the bluffs grew louder.

I recognized the cabin immediately when we arrived, and I was so filled with excitement that I trotted to the front door, dragging their foggy bodies behind me. The front door was propped half open, and there was a light shining from within. Someone was inside. Waiting. My heart sang out, for I knew it was Galen! We would finally be reunited with our offspring.

I pushed my way through the opened door, but as my left foot crossed the threshold, the children vanished from my grip, and I was left alone standing in the foyer. A twinge of dread filled me, and I called out, "Galen?" with a stammering cry. There was no response. The layout of the place was still fresh in my mind, so I ventured into the back kitchen area, and there he was! Cross-legged at the kitchen table. A single candle burned in the center, and next to it, the *Blodheksa* book lay unmolested. He looked as devilishly handsome as the night he appeared to me in my dream.

"Where were you?" I bellowed.

He stood up and outstretched his arms to greet me.

I rushed into his arms, and he enveloped me in a strong embrace—swallowed me up in his reverend's cloak and clasped his arms tightly around my back. I melted into his arms and chest, feeling the beat of his heart against my cheek, and nuzzling my face on the material of his cotton shirt. The tears came before I had a chance to stop them, and I descended into a wave of heaving sobs. "Where were you? Why did you leave me? Why did you abandon me? Us?" I balled up a fist and weakly struck his chest. "You could have saved me! You could have saved them! Do you know what they did? Do you know?"

I was dizzy, frantic, hysterical, but Galen reached his arm up and pet the back of my head in long, soothing strokes. "Easy, easy," he coaxed. "I did protect you. Trust me, Barbara, I did not abandon you. I had to leave for you to *become*."

I pulled back from his grip to look at him. "Become?"

Chapter 18

"And what you did was glorious!" he beamed. "So glorious that you burnt your mark on all of time. You still run hot with revenge. Can't you feel it? The fires that consumed the babies, the fires that consumed the town—it all runs inside you. It breathes in you now and pokes at your veins like thorns from a fiery rose bush. You burn red and orange and yellow, but red most of all, for the red was what licked your soul at its core and branded you with vengeance." He ran his hand down my back, sending my body into a tingling twitch. My eyes fluttered, and for a second, I saw flashes of flames and heard screams in the distance. For a second, I was filled with flames that begged to be released from my fingertips. I swallowed hard and calmed myself back to reality.

"But David. Gretchen," I whispered, a lump forming in my throat again. "Why didn't you stop them?"

"I couldn't. It was far too late. What happened, happened. Like it has in the past, like it will happen again in the future."

I pushed myself off his chest, breaking our embrace. "I don't understand!" I yelled. "I don't understand why my children, *our children*, had to be some sort of sacrifice. Some sort of offering!"

"You do understand, though, Barbara. You've always understood." He extended his arm and reached for me. "You're the Blodheksa, until you aren't," he repeated the words Goody Olson said to me in the jail cell, only he didn't say them out loud. He said them with his inside voice that only

235

I could hear—the voice of the ancients, the voice with the gravelly tone and in the language of long ago. He turned to the table, picked up the book, and handed it to me. "It is yours," he said solemnly. "It has always been yours." I remembered Goody Olson saying those words to me not so long ago.

And suddenly it became so clear: The Blood Witch brings the Blood Brother and the Blood Sister into the world so that the three can bring about the New Eden. "But what are *you*?" I ask in confusion. "You are neither Witch, nor Brother, nor Sister."

"I am but a conduit, Barbara," he says in my mind. "A vehicle of guidance for the Blodheksa. I was yours."

"Goody Olson? She was the Blood Witch?"

"For a time. And then she wasn't."

"Am I the Blodheksa now?"

He shakes his head. "You were. But you are no longer."

I understood. I couldn't be. My children existed, but they were no longer flesh and blood in this world. I nodded my head and kept my gaze on the book's cover.

"Then what am I if not the Blodheksa? What is to become of me?"

"You still have an important role to play, Barbara. Your power is too strong to just fade away into oblivion. You are the Witch. A title not to be taken with little regard. For you are the Witch who brought peace to your sisters as they hanged for what others considered sinful acts. For you are the Witch who was blessed in the clearing of the Black Wood, baptized in red thorns from the start. Your blood blessed the sacred soil and allowed me to find you. For you are the Witch who brought forth the twins—a duo with such supreme power that even death could not contain their essence. You are the Witch they could not burn. Instead, you absorbed their fires of damnation and became one with vengeance."

"So, we can be together now, right? If you are my conduit, we can try again, right? Our great powers can combine once more—here, in this cottage! We can begin again!" My voice sounded pitiful with my inquiry.

He placed his hands on my shoulders lovingly. "I'm afraid not," he said. "That's not how it works. We are on different paths now."

I looked to him sharply as a wave of panic took over my heart. "What do you mean 'different paths?' You're leaving me?" I was frantic. Panicked. The thought of not being with him seized me in a block of ice and temporarily extinguished the fire in my blood.

"I have guided you as much as I can, for you have reached the height of your potential. There are others out there who will need me. Others who need their own powers to be unlocked and realized. Others who have called out to me from ages hence and ages forward. Others who have reached through from their black circles and beckoned me to assist."

"The next Blodheksa?" I said, and the jealousy ran from my tongue.

He chuckled. "Perhaps. Possibly. It is probable. I actually anticipate it to be so."

I jerked my body from his touch and furrowed my brow. "So, you'll be a conduit for some other Witch?" Images sprang to my mind as I spat out the words. Carnal images of Galen mounting a beautiful young woman in the throes of passion. My blood boiled at the thought of him with another.

"Embellish!" he exclaimed with a laugh. "I was but a conduit for one Blood Witch, and that was you and you alone. Besides, you have other things to concern yourself with, Barbara." He looked at the book and back to my eyes. "You will spend the rest of your days figuring out how to get back what they stole from you."

A rustling noise fluttered in the darkness from the corner of the room. Faintly, I could see the outlines of the shadows and my heart skipped a beat. I longed for them. I yearned for them. My precious little ones snuffed away too soon.

Galen leaned in and whispered in my ear, "Your children. Make them flesh again."

"How?" I wailed. "That could take forever!"

He grabbed one end of the book and pulled me closer to him. He dipped his head down and gave me a long, passionate kiss. I swooned and nearly collapsed at the knees.

"Tell me how I can bring them back?" I whispered breathlessly.

Chapter 18

"You have the power. Right here," he shook the book in our hands, "and right here," he pressed one hand to my chest. "You are like me now, and the answers you seek are for you to discover. You have all of earthly eternity to figure it out."

He leaned in again and kissed me harder. Longer. Deeper. I knew that was the kiss of goodbye. The kiss of farewell. Until we met again.

"Will I see you again?" I cried.

"In time. All in good time. When our children are made flesh and blood again, and I have consecrated all my darkly angels, I will find you. Until that time has come, I will be the trespasser from the Black Wood, he who brings the flood in his wake."

"Trent," I declared.

"And you will be the beautiful foreign woman who will wrap her children close to her in her thorn bush and strike deadly if provoked."

"Thorne," I affirmed.

With a final, baptismal kiss to the forehead and a squeeze of my shoulders, Galen sidestepped me and left the cabin.

Left me.

Left the children.

But I knew I was now on a path that would lead me to ultimate glory. With the Blodheksa book in hand, and the shadow children giggling happily in the room, I was determined to fulfill the command my conduit made of me. *Make the children flesh.* If it took me a moon cycle, a year, a decade, a lifetime, or all of eternity, so be it.

I would travel the world, learn all I could, and pursue the one and only goal that mattered.

I looked out the window of the cottage and saw the twisted bramble of a rose bush creeping up to the ledge. I flung the casing up wide and reached out to touch it, to deliberately prick my palm on the sharp little spikes. Three bubbles of blood bloomed up under my flesh and I smiled. One for the Blodheksa, one for the Blodbrødre, one for the Blodsøster. Only that wasn't us. Not anymore. We were something different. We had become something different. And I was determined to spend the rest of my life figuring that out. I breathed in the early winter air. We would need to get moving soon, but I wanted to take it all in one last time before Barbara Thorne introduced herself to the world again. I pressed my hand around the branch and let the prickly sting of the spikes inject themselves in my grip. I squeezed hard and let a palm full of blood rain down upon the rose bush — staining the leaves, staining the base of the flower petals, blessing this domain as my safe spot of protection. The green plant, now painted with my blood. Marked with the magic of my essence. The children giggled again. The sound of their laughter filled me with delight, and in that moment, I felt the memory of Galen begin to fade, and I began to relax with a new purpose and focus.

With my children by my side, I was one with the Red Thorn.

I was the Red Thorn.

I am the Witch of the Red Thorn.

Book Club Questions

1. Nature seems to be a constant presence in Barbara's life. She often describes the moon, the trees, the weather, the feeling of the air and darkness. How is nature significant in Barbara's experiences?

2. Sexual encounters are intertwined with Barbara's other experiences. How is sex important in Barbara's awakening as well as the opening of the portal?

3. Witches, much like ordinary women, can exist independently or within a sisterhood of sorts. Discuss the role of women both within the historical backdrop of the story as well as the story of Barbara's life and her relationship with other women.

4. What growth do you see in Barbara throughout the book?

5. Discuss the role of (Tansy) Temperance in Barbara's trajectory.

6. What is the significance of the twins?

7. Explain the importance of the necklace Barbara wants to take from the hanged witch in Salem. How does it impact her and her relationships?

8. In Chapter 15 Tansy shouts "A book for a witch!" Why is the book important? Why is the town so fixated on it, beyond the idea that it contains witchcraft?

9. A series of dead animals appear throughout the book. Why? What is the significance of each animal (cats, goats, and crows)?

10. The number three is used multiple times. Galen mentions it, the dead animals appear three times, and three people important to Barbara's life are put under her spell. Why the number three?

11. If you have read any of the other books in the series, how was this similar or different to the others? What connections can be made?

Author Bio:

Maria is the author of the Amazon best-selling series *The Coal Elf Chronicles*, *The Altered Experience,* and *The Aestrangel Trinity*. When not writing about dark fantasy and horror, she teaches Language Arts and Journalism to middle school students in Florida. A lover of all things dark and demented, she takes pleasure in warping the comfort factor in her readers' minds. Just when you think you've reached a safe space in her stories, she snaps you back into her twisted reality.

More books from
4 Horsemen Publications

Horror, Thriller, & Suspense

Alan Berkshire
Jungle
Hell's Road

Erika Lance
Jimmy
Illusions of Happiness
No Place for Happiness
I Hunt You

Maria DeVivo
Witch of the Black Circle
Witch of the Red Thorn
Witch of the Silver Locust

Witch of the
White Serpernt

Mark Tarrant
The Mighty Hook

October Kane
Nothing Will Be Left
Everything Will Burn

Steve Altier
The Camping Trip
Jimmy's Curse
The Ghost Hunter

Discover more at
4HorsemenPublications.com